# A CHRISTMAS SONG

## A RYAN'S BED AND SPIN-OFF HOLIDAY NOVELLA

## TIJAN

Copyright © 2023 by TIJAN

Edited by Paige Maroney Smith
Proofread by Kimberely Holm, Chris O'Neil Parece,
Michele Ficht, Amy English

This book has mentions of suicide and a reference to sexual assault. All
locations and a drug is fictitious.

# 1

## MAREN

Where the fuck was I?

I pushed up, sitting up, and everything was aching in me. It's the hangover of all hangovers, and. . . I looked around. Jesus. Seriously. Where *was* I?

This wasn't Jude's room—I saw Cris' basketball jersey.

Fuck.

I was in my ex's room. Although, Cris Chavez and I had never really been in a relationship. We would hook up. Then he would ignore me...until we would hook up again.

The door opened and the smell of coffee hit me right before my stomach pushed up something else to my throat. "Mornin—"

I flung back the blanket and ran for the bathroom. Apparently, he had his own. I fell to my knees, and seeing Cris coming in behind me, I kicked his door shut right as I let loose with the first upheaval in my stomach.

"Hey!" He pounded on the door. "Come on, Maren. Let me in."

God.

Jesus.

Shit.

What had I done? Honest to God asking here. I looked down at myself, seeing I wasn't in the clothes I—what had I *done* last night?

"Maren!" He pounded on the door again.

I ignored him.

It'd been my go-to for handling so much other stuff in my life. Just shut up. Keep it moving. Head down. Survive.

So far it'd been working, but this? Cris? Did we fuck last night?

Jesus. Jude.

Jude! He had a gig last night. I went to the bar with Amber and Toya. We partied beforehand, but that'd been the usual. Nothing new there. I couldn't remember past pre-partying at Toya's. We were drinking. She pulled out some other things, but they partook. I didn't. I stayed away from drugs. I had enough issues to handle. I didn't need to add another one, but I was trying to remember. . . I'd been in a car. We were going to the bar. I was in the back and that was it.

I didn't remember anything past that.

What the hell?

My body chilled at the same time panic seared me.

"Come on, Maren. Come out. I want to talk to you."

I shut it all down, I had to. It'd been my go-to for just getting through life lately, but once I was done throwing up, I looked under Cris' cabinet. He usually kept an extra toothbrush somewhere.

Found it.

He and I hadn't been exclusive, but I got to know him from whatever we had been. I mean, the first time I saw him making out with a girl at a party, I'd felt kicked in the stomach, but I got my act together after that. We were in the NCAA division for basketball and Cris was on the team, a starting player. He wasn't one of their best two players, but he was in the solid top five. He was their best power forward. I'd been ecstatic when we first started hooking up. His roommate and my roommate were already dating. Cris was hot. He seemed to like me. It made sense, but stupid me, I thought we'd been exclusive until. . . Yeah. Until I learned differently.

Ugh. Here I was, thinking about the past when I had real shit to handle.

After quickly brushing my teeth, I grimaced when I looked at myself. Pale. God. I changed my hair color to black with blue highlights. I was always a strawberry blonde type and I liked wearing make-up, but I blended last year. There was nothing that stood out about me. Typical party girl and when I changed my hair, I wanted to change everything. I started going darker with my make-up and though I usually enjoyed the smokey eye look, it was not looking so good this morning. I might need to rethink my make-up choices.

I tried to do what I could with my hair, and washed my face clean.

Cris started to pound on the door again when I thrust it open.

His eyes widened, his hand in mid-knock, and he blinked at me. "Hi."

I scowled, brushing past him.

"Uh—what? Hey!"

*I couldn't be here.*

*I could not be here.*

That was on repeat in my head as I rushed around his room, looking for my things. My clothes. My purse. My phone?

"Hey!"

There was nothing here. I rounded on him. "Where's my shit?"

Cris looked at me for a second before anger flared and he scowled at me. "Are you fucking kidding me?"

"Where's my stuff, Chavez?" I huffed again, my hands on my

hips. "You can't take my things and keep them from me. Where are they?"

There was a tick of silence, and I looked away.

I couldn't stare at him, not when he was getting pissed right back at me.

I'd forgotten how hot Cris was. He was six five. Wide shoulders. Lean frame, but he had some bulk on him. It's why they made him a power forward. He was good at shoving his way around under the basket. Brown skin that sometimes was so sleek and smooth when he was sweating that he made me want to lick every inch of him. Black hair that he was letting grow out a little this year. It'd been kept short last year, almost a crew cut. This year, he had enough where it was messily rumpled, and I got one look and my vagina was remembering the last time we fucked.

What was wrong with me?

"Are you fucking kidding me?" he growled, those eyes heated and smoldering.

My clit twitched.

Fuck.

"I said—"

"I know what the fuck you said," he unloaded. "I don't have your shit because you didn't have any shit with you."

I frowned.

He took a step toward me. "Want to know the state we found you in?"

We?

"You were on the ground. You were so fucking drunk that you couldn't sit in the chair." Another step. He was still seething. "And your buddies with you, what a couple of *great* friends you have. They did nothing. Goddamn fucking nothing. You're on your ass and they're watching the band. And they kept doing nothing when I came over, picked you up off your ass, and carried you out of there."

I winced hearing that. I wasn't altogether surprised, but it was a little hard to hear at the same time.

"Want to know who else saw me throw you over my shoulder and did nothing about it?"

I frowned, my mouth drying up.

Another step and now he was breathing down his nose at me. His hands were in fists at his side. "Your fucking boyfriend."

Another grimace.

"Yeah," he bit out. "He saw the whole thing. You falling. You not getting back up. Your friends not helping. And a guy coming over and hauling you out of there."

It didn't look good, but I shrugged. "He probably thought you were security—"

"THEN HE SHOULD'VE MADE SURE!"

I jerked, backing away.

Cris cursed, raking a hand through his hair. "Sorry. I—just —I could've been anyone. Any guy could've taken you out of there. Does he know we used to hook up?"

Another flinch from me because the truth was that Jude and I spoke very little. That was part of the attraction. It was why Amber, Toya, and I hung out too. They didn't care.

They didn't ask questions.

I could get through the day then.

But here Chavez was, getting in my face, not knowing the score. I shook my head, looking away. "I didn't have anything with me?"

He was still glaring, and that was not what he wanted me to say. He bit back another growl before he exploded again. "Are you fucking with me? Actually fucking with me—"

I snapped, "Shut up! SHUT UP! You know nothing. You don't ask anything. You're just judging and—" I paled, realizing what I just did. Cris would ask questions now. I couldn't have that. I'd break if anyone started caring.

"Can I use your phone?"

His eyes narrowed. "What for?"

"Because if I didn't have anything with me, then either Jude has them or I left them in Amber's car. Also, I need a ride."

"I'll give you a ride."

"What? No—"

"Only goddamn way you're getting my phone to call around looking for your shit."

I glared. "Cris."

His eyes turned a whole new level of loathing. He wouldn't budge. I recognized that look on his face.

I bit out, "Fine."

"Fine." He slapped his phone into my hand and I paused, my face lighting up because I only had three numbers memorized. Cris', my roommate's, and my old childhood landline. All that I couldn't use.

"Shit," slipped out.

Cris rolled his eyes, picking up his keys. "Yeah. That's what I thought." He went over and opened the door. "After you."

I wore his sweatshirt, his shorts, and I had nothing on my feet. Well, okay then.

I sailed right past him.

## 2

# MACKENZIE

There was a brief knock at Ryan's door. He padded barefoot from his bathroom and opened it, then stepped back, opening it wider. Chavez stuck his head inside, scanning over both of us with a slight grimace. "You guys heard?"

Ryan snorted, going to pull on one of his Macquire basketball sweatshirts and sticking his hands in the front pocket. "I think everyone heard. Take it the talk didn't go so well?"

I was still in bed, but was sitting up with my knees pulled to my chest. When we heard the yelling from beneath us, there'd been no way I could've gone back to bed. Ryan got up for the bathroom, and I slipped out to grab one of his shirts before crawling back in bed. I'd been rooted in place, trying to make out the rest of what was being said from his room. Not all of the words were audible.

"What'd you guys hear?"

Ryan glanced my way before answering, "Mostly a lot of curse words."

Chavez flicked his eyes upwards, stepping more into the doorway, his hand on the doorknob. "She's a fucking mess. Literally, but I'm taking her around to find where her things are. And speaking of," his gaze turned my way, "you don't have an extra key for your place, do you? She needs new clothes, and she has no way of getting into your place."

"Of course, yeah." A pang sliced through me because she hadn't messaged me asking for the extra copy herself. "Does she know I was there last night?"

"No. She's not brought up anyone's names. She's just mad at me."

"What'd she say when you told her about how her boyfriend did nothing when you carried her out of the bar?"

His gaze hardened. "She said nothing."

I started to reach for my own keys, but paused at that answer. Jesus. What was going on with Maren?

Ryan came over, touched a hand to my shoulder. "I'll give him my key. We can make an extra later today."

"Oh, okay." I frowned, looking at Chavez again. "Does she know I'm up here?"

His mouth thinned. "She looked around in the living room once, but that was it. She's not said anything, asked anything. The girl's in her own world, but something is going on."

Ryan had taken his key off his own set and handed it over. "Let us know when you know?"

"Of course." Chavez took the key, pocketing it, and his gaze returned to me. "I'm going to let her know that you're the one who went looking for her."

I froze, unsure if I wanted her to know that.

Ryan's eyes narrowed.

Chavez shot him a look, shaking his head briefly. "Don't worry. I'm going to lay it on thick how Mac was there looking out for her, because she was worried, because she cares, because she's a good fucking friend, what Maren is very much not doing right now."

"Don't..." I started, but then paused because ugh. This

whole situation was somewhat messed up. "I should just go down there and talk to her myself."

Ryan moved forward a step, but Chavez said, "No. Let me handle her. She's in a mood. Let me be the one she's pissed at. She won't get mad at you, Mac. I've never seen her mad or irritated at you. All the time we were hooking up, she never said anything negative about you. Even a normal frustration. If you go down there, she might not be able to help herself and I know her. She'll regret later saying anything unkind toward you. She needs to fight."

That made sense, but I frowned. I didn't like it. I didn't like not going to my friend even though everything he said was the smart thing to do. "I'm going to call her later, though. This afternoon."

He nodded slowly. "Wait until after two." He asked Ryan, "You're heading to class soon?"

Ryan looked at the clock. "Yeah. I'll go in early, take Mac to her class, and wait around until our class at ten. You're skipping?"

Chavez gestured behind him with his head. "I'll handle her first and go from there."

The two jerked up their chins toward each other before Chavez left, shutting the door behind him.

Ryan eyed me, not moving from where he was still standing. "What's in your head?"

I shook my head, lying down and curling on my side.

Ryan slid in next to me, pulling me over to him so our legs tangled together. His hand went through my hair. It was lighter again, so I was back to the golden blonde color that Willow and I shared for so much of our lives. I was getting older, but I wanted to believe that our faces would've remained identical always. Heart-shaped chins. Slender arms. Long legs. Though, I wanted to put more muscle on my frame. We used to be petite.

I closed my eyes now, savoring that touch from Ryan.

I said, almost in a whisper, "I feel bad that I've not been there for her."

"Stop." Ryan pulled me to him, rolling to his back and he tugged me on top of him. His one hand cupped the back of my head, our eyes meeting, as his other went to my hip, kneading. "You both got busy. She got a new boyfriend. And you were dealing with your stuff this summer. You can only do so much, Mac. Taking care of yourself and me is enough, I think."

"I know, but—"

He shook his head. "No. Stop it."

I frowned and scrambled up, but only so I was straddling him. I sank down on him, as both of his hands went to my hips, then sliding down my legs and back up. "No, listen. Maren is one of my only friends from college and she's my roommate. I should've known something was going on."

His mouth flattened, even as I began rolling over him, slowly, and he was helping guide me, pulling me down over him tightly. "No. She got a boyfriend. That's normal. She's barely been around, so how would you have known? You've been handling your own stuff, me, and college. And making sure your parents feel appeased with you. Taking on your roommate's shit, that's not on you. You take too much on and you might relapse, or whatever the word is, and that can't happen. No fucking way. You're up here beating yourself up when Maren's not been a good friend to you."

Tendrils of pleasure were shooting up my spine, as I began moving harder over him, grinding and holding, but there was some truth in what he said. I tipped my head back, my eyes closed, as I murmured, starting to pant slightly, "She was probably lost in her own shit. Just like I was."

"I don't care," Ryan said huskily as he sat up, his arm clamped around my back so I remained in place, but he tugged off my shirt, his other hand running up my side. "I also don't give any fucks about your roommate at this moment." His eyes were lidded, heavy with lust as his mouth closed over one of my breasts. His tongue lapped around my nipple.

That felt so good.

I kept rolling over him, groaning as Ryan moved his mouth to my other breast before he tugged my head down, my mouth opening over his. After that, there was no more conversation. It wasn't long before he lifted me up and both of us tugged his pants down. I hadn't been wearing underwear or pants under his shirt, so when he pulled me back down, we both groaned as he slipped inside of me.

God, I loved my man.

I loved how he made me feel.

I loved riding him, and knowing exactly how hard I could go because he loved all of it.

I pushed him down, a hand to his chest, and I leaned back, my eyes closed, my back arched as I moved over him, taking him in deep and fast and rough, and this was all me this morning.

Ryan groaned, his hands gripping my thighs until it started to get too much for him. He pressed a thumb to my clit, rubbing me, and I cried out. "Agh—asshole. Not yet." But my protest was breathy and ended on a laugh.

He ignored me, pressing harder before his other hand moved behind me, circling my other hole back there.

"Ryan!" I moaned, grabbing his hand and holding it hostage for a moment.

He chuckled, before he continued circling me still under my hand, and I didn't do anything to stop him. I couldn't. I didn't want to because my climax was starting.

I held still, feeling it move up my spine until I erupted, my body jerking forward. His thumb kept rounding over my clit, pressing in.

I cried out, cursing.

He held me up as I started to fall off of him, keeping me in place as the waves crashed over me until they began to subside. When my body stopped trembling, Ryan flipped us so he was on top. I opened my eyes, my lids too heavy, but saw his own staring deep into mine, molten.

Those hazel eyes of his. How they could go so dark, I didn't know, but they took my breath away. Along with his square jaw, the dimple in his right cheek. He was more ripped since coming to college, and I felt the power in his body right now. It was exhilarating.

Then he began to thrust into me, and really thrust.

Hard. Deep.

He let out a guttural growl, bending over me, his lips finding my throat. "You feel so fucking good, Mac. So tight."

I moaned with him, lifting one of my legs to wrap around him.

He caught it, going deeper into me somehow, and it wasn't long until I felt a second release starting to build.

"This is mine," he panted, fucking me. He pressed a hand where we were joined, lifting his head so he could watch as he moved inside of me. "My pussy. Mine." His eyes met mine, so heated. "You're mine."

His words, mixed with how he was looking at me, claiming me, and the sensations he was building back up inside of me were too much.

I came again, and he continued riding me through my second release until at the very end, I felt him unloading with me. He clamped down around me, his mouth breathing into my neck. "My woman."

I ran a hand up his back, whispering back, "You're mine too."

He lifted his head, his lips finding mine. "Fuck yeah, I am." We kissed until he lifted his head back up. "Want to keep you here the rest of the fucking day."

I grinned against his lips as they'd fallen back to mine and said, still against them, "Can't. Classes. Practice."

"Fuck all of that." He captured my throat in his hand and arched over me, sealing his mouth to mine in a hot kiss. Demanding more from me. He was kissing me as if he really was going to keep me in bed for the rest of the day, but he wouldn't. He couldn't, and knowing my man, I was happy to let him kiss me as long as he wanted until he jumped out of bed, lifting me with him, and he took me to the shower.

After that, he slid back inside of me one more time before we both had to rush getting dressed and getting to campus.

I wasn't a fan of being late, but as I slid into my seat right as the professor walked in, it'd been worth it.

# 3

## MAREN

I glared at Cris when I saw that he'd taken me to my dorm.
"What are we doing here? I told you Jude's address. That's
where I've been staying."

He shrugged, turning off his truck and getting out. "Figured
you could hit the refresh button. Get some clothes from here
and then we can go and find where your other stuff is."

"My computer is at Jude's."

He didn't respond, just shut his door and walked around the
front, waiting for me.

Fine. Fucking fine. I got out, shut his door, and strode ahead
of him, ignoring how I was barefoot. The clothes I'd had on the
night before were put in a bag, and he handed me the bag
when we left his house. He ran upstairs and I wasn't an idiot. I
knew he was going up to talk to Ryan Jensen, my roommate's
boyfriend. It'd been on the tip of my tongue to ask if Mac was
in there with him. My first ever roommate and my first ever best
friend. I'd not talked to her, not really for so long, and being
around Cris was driving me crazy. He was bringing up old
memories, old feelings. The four of us hung out so much

together. We'd had our own little world inside this crazy college experience.

It'd been nice.

Talking to Mac.

Laughing with her.

It felt right, easy being with her.

We trusted each other, which was a big deal.

Ryan was one of the best basketball players, Cris not far behind, so it felt like the world wanted in on what we had. That made it feel so much more special than it really had been, or that's how I felt the first time I saw Chavez hooking up with someone who wasn't me. So I couldn't miss those times because what I felt hadn't been totally true. But I did miss Mac. I hadn't talked to her in so long. It felt like forever.

I started to ask, but Cris came back down and he gave me a haughty superior smirk, knowing I wanted to ask, so I swallowed that up right away.

Once I got my phone, I'd call her. She should know what was going on with me.

When I needed to tune everything out, including my feelings, I stopped hooking up with Cris, and that led me to tuning Mac out at the same time. I needed to do that in the beginning because it was too much. I couldn't keep my shit together, but I was better now. Or I had more of a handle on things so I *could* talk to my roommate. I wouldn't get eaten alive by all the other feelings.

He followed me upstairs, right as a door opened on my hallway. I kept going, but a girl said, "Oh, hey man."

Cris held back, and as I got to my room, I looked over my shoulder. He was talking to a girl, who was eyeing me at the same time. I didn't know her, but Cris seemed chummy with her.

I tried my door, but it was locked.

Which meant Mac had been at the house because she

should've still been here. Her morning class wasn't for another fifty minutes. She only left early enough to grab coffee or food because people sometimes recognized her as Jensen's girlfriend and she liked to avoid that attention.

"Yo," Cris said.

I looked his way.

He tossed something my way. Taking a few steps forward, I caught it, seeing it was a key.

I paused, a weird sensation prickling the back of my neck. "Was this Mac's?"

"Ryan's."

I couldn't move for a moment, needing to know. "Was she there this morning?"

He tilted his head up, a knowing smirk showing again. He raised an eyebrow.

That was my answer. My body got hot. Anger started to flood me. "Was she there last night too? At the bar?"

The girl's eyes got big, the one standing next to him. She was looking between him and me, but she didn't say anything.

"Go and get dressed. Clean up. I'll wait and then we can have another whole discussion about what happened last night." He looked at the girl, moving with his back to me. It was a clear dismissal, and something about it made me grit my teeth.

The girl edged back a step, so she could still see me, and those eyes only got bigger.

I frowned. Something about her was familiar. Not that she lived on this same floor as Mac and me, but something else.

But, shaking that off, I went inside and drew in a breath to calm my nerves.

Mac's laptop was in the room. She wouldn't mind me using it. I booted it up, used the password for the account she assigned to me in case I ever needed to use it, and I sent Jude a DM.

**Do you have my phone? Or my purse?**

It read 'seen' right away, but he didn't type back.

I sent the same message to Amber and Toya in their DMs.

Amber was the only one who typed back right away.

**Yeah. You left your purse at Troy's. It's still there. I don't know about your phone. Want me to ask Troy to check your purse? See if it's in there?**

When had we gone to Troy's? He was Luis' boyfriend, the drummer in Jude's band. I bit back a curse because I had no idea if I would've taken my phone with me. If I'd been wasted enough, and if someone had distracted me, I might've left it behind in my purse. Though, I was pretty conditioned to keep my phone with me.

Maybe it was in Cris' truck? Might've fallen out of my jeans?

I replied to Amber, **Could you check your backseat? See if my phone is there? Maybe fell out or something.**

**Amber: Sure will. I'm just leaving to pick Toya up for coffee and breakfast with the guys. Want me to swing over and get you?**

Oh! I was tempted, really tempted. Cris hadn't come barging in here. It'd be easy to slip out through the exit at the end of the hall, but I would still need to check his truck for my phone. Why hadn't I thought about it on the way here in the first place?

I wrote back, **No. I need to check somewhere first and then I'll get a ride to Troy's.**

**Amber: Okay. Check Troy's bedroom when you get there. Sometimes he takes our things in there so his roommates don't go through them.**

**Me: Good call. I'll talk to you later.**

I looked at Jude and Toya's messages. Both had seen my message. Neither replied.

Awesome.

Cris' sarcastic words haunted me. ". . .what a couple of *great* friends you have."

We weren't actually friends. We wasted time together while sharing the same pursuit of either being numb or being wasted so we didn't feel anything else.

But it bugged me that Jude and Toya didn't respond.

Maybe there was something to what Cris said, and I needed to. . . No. I was aware of the situation. He wasn't. He could go eat a dick for all I cared.

I had no doubt I'd share that sentiment with him the next time he got in my face, because he was so eager for another showdown. I'd forgotten that Cris liked fighting. It'd been foreplay for us in the beginning until we just skipped fighting and went straight to banging. Even now, I grew heated barely thinking about a few of those times.

I cursed, shutting down Mac's laptop and going to grab my things for a shower. My body trembled a little bit too, and I couldn't lie to myself, saying that it was left over from my hangover. It was Cris and remembering how it felt when he'd pound inside of me.

He wasn't talking to that girl when I went to the bathroom, but he was waiting still outside her door, which was almost directly across from the bathroom door.

He watched me walk toward him, his dark eyes going almost black the closer I got, his eyes trailing up and down over me, warming me with each pass of his eyes.

I got to the door, both of us paused, and the hallway had shrunk in size. It was only him. Only me.

Fuck. I wanted him.

He straightened, reading what I felt, and his eyes flashed, the same hunger showing right back.

My mouth watered, but I forced myself to go into the bathroom.

There was no one else inside.

My limbs turned leaden, and I went on autopilot, knowing what I really wanted to do, not letting myself think about it. He thought Jude was my boyfriend. I knew so many did, but that wasn't the situation. And as I waited for the water to heat, I was barely feeling it.

Everything in me tightened up in need. I was aching for Cris, literally aching.

Jesus.

Why was this happening now? It's like when I woke up in his bed, it woke the other part of me that I'd been trying to keep dead. I couldn't handle it, but then I was moving without making a conscious decision.

I left my stall door open.

I went to the bathroom door, pushed it open.

Cris was there.

My gaze went right to his, and he'd been waiting.

We shared a look, just one before he pushed off from the wall, and caught the door as I began heading back to my shower stall.

He was right on my tail, a hand on my back, almost pushing me forward.

Then the door was shut, locked, and he pushed me against the far wall. As I turned around, neither of us said a word. His mouth was on mine, and I answered him, sagging into him, and everything in my body was yelling out, "Yessssss."

My clothes were pulled off, tossed onto the bench in the corner.

His were tugged off right after. His shoes. Everything was put on the same bench. He grabbed a condom from his wallet, then picked me up and walked me into the shower part. My back hit the wall. My legs wound around his back, and it wasn't long before he had the condom on, his dick sheathed inside of me.

God.

It'd been so long.

Too long.

A part of me had missed this.

When this was over, I'd have to do some work to put that part of me asleep all over again. But until then, I began moving my hips over Cris as he was pounding into me, doing what we'd done in the past when we needed to fuck but we needed to be quiet. Our mouths were either on top of each other or we had our hands over each other's mouth because sometimes, being quiet was hard. It was *damn* hard.

Today was the hardest it'd ever been.

## 4

## MACKENZIE

A girl was waiting for me when I left my first class. She jumped up from a bench, hurrying to me. "Mackenzie! Hey."

I paused, skimming her over. I didn't know her. Auburn hair with blonde highlights. Big wire glasses set over hazel eyes. Caucasian. A little shorter than me with a stocky body type. She was wearing cover-alls that were made from some soft fabric and a t-shirt underneath. A necklace hung down from her neck with a single pearl at the end. She looked comfortable and trendy.

"Hi...?"

She held her hand out, a bright smile on her face. "My name is Kellie Rispins. I'm a blogger at Hoops & Secret Scoops. I cover a lot of different topics for the university. Do you have a minute? Could I ask you some questions?" She handed me her business card.

A blogger.

This happened a lot the first year, when they tried getting to me before I caught on to what they wanted. Mostly, they were friendly. They wanted to interview Ryan Jensen's girlfriend.

They meant well, wanted to portray me or us in a positive light, but there'd been some who had the 'gotcha' angle behind their blogs. They wanted dirt, and Ryan being as big of a basketball player as he was, they thought his name would jumpstart their career.

She had that look. It was small, and it was hidden well, but it was there.

I shook my head. "No comment." I ignored her after that, heading outside and beginning to angle my way to check the mail area.

She caught up to me, a hand to my arm. "I'm not here to do you bad or anything, but you need to know something."

I paused, but gave her hand a meaningful look.

She snatched it away, shuffling out of the way of oncoming people. Lowering her head and voice, she tucked a strand of her hair behind her ear, saying, "I had to ask. What kind of journalist would I be if I didn't, but I get it. I do. But, listen, you should know that a bunch of us got tips dropped in our DMs by a credible source saying that you were seeking treatment in a mental health facility this summer."

My body went cold.

"Most times, mental health is off-limits, but we're being told your treatment has been affecting Jensen's playing. What affects Ryan Jensen, affects the team, and that is what everyone is mostly concerned about. So, do you have any comment that your mental health struggles have affected Ryan Jensen's playing this year?"

This was a nightmare. It wasn't my worst-case scenario, but it was up there. What I struggled with, had struggled with in the past was considered taboo. People didn't want to hear about it. They didn't want to hear the word that was used to describe it. Somehow, it got mixed up with other words and phrases like weak, giving up, coward. The truth *was so much the opposite*. Struggling with what I did, what Willow did, it was the hardest struggle to endure. It was crippling. It was a burden no one else could understand, and that was if they even wanted to understand.

For this girl to stand in front of me, ask me so casually, almost carelessly, about how my mental health was affecting Ryan? I wanted to sink my teeth into her neck and never let go.

She was waiting, watching me with an eagerness that had my blood boiling.

I took a breath and counted to ten.

*God, Willow, if you were here? What would you say to this girl?*

My sister would rip into her and wouldn't let loose until she had to crawl away, permanently scarred.

She'd been watching me process her question, and the longer it took me to say anything, the slight smug look she first had was beginning to fade.

"Off the record," I started, flashing her a forced smile because I was not stupid. I knew how this worked. If she was calling herself a journalist, she would need to adhere to their code. Off the record meant nothing I said could be used. When that smug expression completely fell away, I continued, my tone chilled, "How did you think this was going to go? You throw out a statement like that, where if it was true, would be when I was at my most vulnerable and you swoop in to do what? Shame me? Guilt me? *If* it were true? Or is this a very crass way of letting me know that someone is targeting my boyfriend already? Their first practice was yesterday. There's no credibility to your source because of that mere fact. You want a scoop? Look at who dropped that tip and find out why they're making up shit."

I began to leave when she called out behind me, "Was any of that a comment?"

I paused again, leveling her with a hard look. "Still off the record here, but I'm assuming you did your research into me. You know what my sister did?" Her eyes flashed. She did. I kept

on, drawing in some air, for what I wasn't sure. Rationality?
Strength? Calm? Either way, I was still gritting my teeth at
dealing with this topic at all. "If you continue down this line of
reporting, I've half a mind to do what my sister would've done."

She frowned.

I pressed my mouth together. "You didn't do enough
research. Willow wasn't nice like me. She was vengeful, so if
you think to try using any possible mental health struggles I
may have against Ryan, I'll do what my sister would've done.
She would've turned the lens on you. She would look into you.
Look into your loved ones. Look for any dirty secrets you may
be holding onto, and then she would've blasted them to the
world so you could see what that might be like, your biggest
vulnerability used as a headline."

Her mouth snapped closed. "You can't do that to all of us."

I shook my head. "There's not many of you that would use
someone's mental health as click bait, and all of that was *still* off
the record."

She held back when I left, and I bypassed the mailroom and
went straight for the library.

Some may say I acted too quickly, that I was on the defense
too soon. They'd be wrong. To have my personal struggle get
used against Ryan? It was something I never wanted to happen.
Ever. And fuck her because how dare she? Come at me,
throwing that rumor in my face? Everything I said was the
truth, including that very little press would use my mental
health for a tagline. But it was also true that the real story was
whoever was already going after Ryan so as I turned on a
computer, I added one of Ryan's teammates to the list for me to
start cyberstalking.

But first, I was going to turn Kellie Rispins's life upside
down and see what shook free.

# 5

# MAREN

Right after we both came, I shoved him off of me, turned my back, and finished my shower. As far as he was concerned, he could go—I didn't know, but I was a mess of whirling emotions once we finished. Or I was until he groaned behind me, a hand slid around my waist and he fit himself to me all over again.

"Don't," I said, going still.

"Right." He scoffed, his body pressing in hard against me. His hand slid up, circled my breast before giving it a squeeze and moving down between my legs. He pressed over my clit, circling me, rubbing, and at the same time, his teeth grazed over my shoulder.

I shuddered in his arms, but gritted my teeth. "What are you doing?"

He began grinding up and into me, and I clamped down on a whimper leaving me. My whole body seized up, and feeling it, Cris picked me up, smashing me against the wall in front of us. His hand left my clit, moving farther south and slid up into me.

God.

He'd just been in there.

I bit down on my lips, a low moan escaping before I could stop it.

His hips were rolling up against me from behind, and he was getting hard again.

He'd been like that when we hooked up. He could go again, almost immediately. Today was proving that was still true. He didn't respond to my question, moving my hair to the side, and he scraped his teeth to the middle of my back, going up, biting down on the back of my neck.

"Jesus—" I burst out, my back arching, or it would've if I'd had any space to move.

My whole body tensed up, and Cris groaned behind me, breathing out, his other hand wedging in front of me to palm one of my breasts, his fingers rolling over my nipple, "Fuck, how can you still feel this good?" I felt him shaking behind me, but he was also growing more insistent. More urgent. He began kissing down my back, my spine. Tasting me as he went until his hands left me, going to my hips and he was kneeling behind me.

He moved my cheeks aside, nudged my feet apart, and his tongue filled me instead.

"Fuck," I breathed out.

"Say that again, baby." He went back to tonguing me, before pulling out and pressing a light kiss to the inside of my thigh. Then his teeth went there and he nipped me.

"Agh!"

"Shhh." He stood back up, grinning against my shoulder. He kicked out my feet farther apart, yanked my hips back, and I felt his cock at my entrance all over again.

We'd just finished and we were going to do it again?

Yes.

Yes, we were.

Desire was blanketing everything in me. I had no rational thought. I just needed him. He'd been a habit that I kicked a year ago, and now he was giving me a taste. I couldn't stop myself from indulging in a second, but I said, my throat so thick, "Condom."

"Fuck." He pulled away, padding out of our shower stall to where our clothes were.

He was back a moment later, running a hand from my clit and out, sliding up between my ass before he angled me for him all over again. Then he thrust in, and we both moaned at the contact.

"You're tight. Did you stay this way for me, baby? Hmmm?" He was moving in and out of me, setting a hard and fast rhythm. This one was meant to be a quickie, but he was forgetting this was my favorite position.

I loved being sprawled out, where I was helpless to move, and where he could dominate me.

I wanted him to go hard, rough, and take his pleasure out on my body.

Because of that, as he began pounding, each stroke designed to almost punish me, I bit down on my lip to keep any of my sounds from leaving. My pulse was a stampede in my body, drowning everything out except the sensations he was giving me, the delicious, sinful, carnal pleasure.

"Fuck," he breathed into my ear, bending over me. "You are soaking. That's for me? Maren? Hmmm. Is it?" He kept pounding into me, rearing back and drilling back in. "I forgot how much you like it this way. I could make you bleed and you'd just keep coming for me, wouldn't you? Your tight pussy that's just for me." He shoved me up higher, lifting me off my feet so he could deliver sharp thrusts up into me, yanking my hips down over him. He was almost animalistic, but it was building. Rising. A release the size of my own tsunami twisted up throughout me, and I yelled out, unable to keep my sounds silenced anymore.

"Shhh." He chuckled before he shoved three fingers into my

mouth. "Wouldn't want your RA to come in and find us, would you?"

I moaned around his fingers, my head falling back against his shoulder.

"I'm going to do such nasty, filthy things to you later. I can't wait, Maren. You're still mine. You know that, right? You were never someone else's. Mine. You've only been mine."

I tensed. I wanted to fight against what he was saying, but a part of me knew that I couldn't. Cris owned my body, and he had no idea that he also owned my heart.

I couldn't let him have that again. No.

Lifting my head, I couldn't do anything else. He had me smashed against the wall, and he was holding me immobile. I was only there for him to do what he wanted to my body. But I could squeeze him inside of me, and I did that, trying to slow him down.

"What are you doing, Maren?" He peppered kisses up my throat, turning my face to meet his. His mouth covered mine, his tongue sweeping in, exploring me that way also. As soon as he pulled away, his fingers filled me up again, but the heat was swirling at the base of my spine.

The tsunami whipped through me in a frenzy and I exploded, fireworks going off inside of me.

He kept thrusting through my release, going faster. Pistoning.

I'd just finished my last wave of my release when I felt him pausing and then unloading inside of me as well.

He chuckled hoarsely behind my ear, "That was take two." He pulled his fingers out, some saliva going with him. He ignored it, his hand smoothing over my face before running down my back, finding my hip. He pulled out, lowering me down.

My knees buckled, but he caught me, a second low chuckle coming from him.

As soon as I could stand on my own, I shoved him away.

He went this time, just to stand to the side, and he used some of my shampoo. He cleaned himself off, rinsing his hair as he watched me the whole time. I had turned my back to the wall, resting there, scowling at him the whole time.

When he was done, he touched my chin, his eyes falling to my mouth and darkening. "I'll wait for you outside."

He left, and I closed my eyes, hating him as tears threatened to leak out of me.

"Oh!" a girl exclaimed.

"Well, hello there." A second one joined, flirtatious.

"Ladies," he drawled. I could hear his smirk in his tone.

A moment later, both girls dissolved into laughs and giggles.

"Who was that?" one breathed out.

"Cristiano Chavez. Starting power forward for our basketball team."

"Uh, okay, Basketball Nerdgirl."

I remained where I was, the shower spray just misting me from my angle. I could hear more girls joining at the sinks. The clinks and thuds of their utility baskets were being moved around. They were getting ready for something, which meant I'd either need to wait them out or walk past them.

"The bigger question is who was in there with him?"

"Shh!" one of them hushed the others.

I let out a sigh, moving to finish my shower.

They were still there when I finished. I could hear their hushed voices now in a low conversation, but fuck them. Fuck being ashamed.

I hadn't brought in a change of clothes, just my towels and Cris had taken one of them, leaving me the other. I growled under my breath, but wrapped it around me, and with the rest of my stuff tucked under my arm, walked out.

Six girls were at the mirrors, and all paused, eyeing me in the mirror.

I met each and every one of their gazes, until one by one they dropped their gazes.

The last one didn't, whirling around to stare at me head-on. She leaned against her sink.

I recognized her from some parties that Jude's band threw at their house.

"We're not supposed to have guys in here," she said to me, haughty.

I moved my back to the door, stepping into it, and met her eyes. I smirked, holding up a middle finger as I pushed through the door. "So report me."

# 6

## MAREN

C ris was waiting in the hallway, dressed, and talking to that girl again.

I felt him watching me, but ignored both of them and went to my room to dress. Checking my Insta, Jude and Toya still hadn't responded to me.

Amber: I checked the back of my car, but nothing there. Troy said your purse is at his house. He moved it into his bedroom, and he said to check his closet. Just inside the door on the right. Jude didn't show up for breakfast, but Luis was there. He said he didn't see anyone carrying your stuff from the bar. Keep me in the loop. I can meet up with you later and help you search.

Amber: Also, Toya is acting weird. Luis and Troy keep glaring at her so I'm wondering if she hooked up with someone she doesn't want us to know about? The theories that are in my head right now. LOL Ok. Bye. We're off to the music store.

This was all annoying, especially having Cris back in my life. How had that happened? I hadn't cared to ask questions this morning because I'd been in half of a panic, just needing to get away from him. He wasn't letting that happen and letting him fuck me, bad move. He'd be insufferable now, but I still needed to search his truck.

He was still talking with that girl when I left the room, pocketing the key and moving their way.

He held out his hand. "I'll take that, thank you very much."

I glared. "It's a key to my room."

"It's Ryan's key, and once we find your things, you'll have your own key back."

I continued glaring at him.

He raised an eyebrow, waving his fingers at me to drop it in his palm. "Come on. If we can't find your stuff, I'll give it back." He cocked his head to the side, so smug, taunting me. "Promise." The crooked grin he flashed me told me he was lying. He wouldn't give me the key, but I also didn't want to stand in the hallway and argue with him.

"Fine," I huffed, slapping it into his hand. He caught my hand before I could yank it away and tugged me to him, turning me around in a smooth move, pulling my back to his front. His arms crossed in front of me.

"Chavez," I growled, a warning.

I felt his chest laughing behind me, but he didn't let it out. "Just relax a moment. Let me introduce you to Lauren here."

The girl had been waiting, watching us until that moment. She held her hand out. "Hi, I'm Lauren. I was at the bar last night."

She had dark brown skin and was wearing a shirt that hugged her curves. Her jeans had paint splotches on them, but the kind where it could've been because she was a painter or because she bought them that way since they looked trendy at the same time. Big bright eyes that were skirting between Cris and me, as she was trying to hold back a grin. Her dreadlocks were pulled back with a hair band so they fell down her back.

I shook her hand, but also felt weird about shaking her

hand. What college student shakes hands with another student? But it seemed normal to her.

"You were at the bar?"

She nodded, eager. "I went with Mac."

I stilled. "You know Mac?"

"We had a class together last year and we got to talking yesterday. You came up in conversation."

I tried taking a step backwards, but Cris was there and his arms tightened. "I came up? How'd I come up?"

Some of her slight grin faded. "We were talking about roommates and she mentioned your boyfriend's name. I have a friend who's obsessed with Hell Skate."

That was Jude's band.

"Oh." Some of the tension faded, until the other part of her statement clicked. It took a nosedive. "Mac saw me like that?" My voice broke.

I missed my roommate. I really missed her.

What had I been doing the last few months?

Lauren and Cris were quiet, letting me process.

"I need to talk to her." An urgent feeling came over me. I needed to see Mac. I needed to talk to Mac *now*. I started to leave as if I could track her down by myself.

Cris got in front of me. His hands lifted, falling to my shoulders. "Wait. Hold up."

"Cris," I managed. My throat swelled up, growing thick. "I have to see her. I have to explain—" Explain what?

There was a reason I stopped seeing Cris.

There was a reason I began hanging out with other people. A different crowd. It'd been a conscious decision.

But, fuck.

It was affecting me that Mac saw me last night, saw how I was. I hadn't been expecting this to hit me how it was, and panic slithered through me.

"Hey, uh." Lauren gentled her voice. "I'm not sure what's all going on, but if you're worried about her thinking a certain way about you, you don't need to worry about that."

"What do you mean?"

"She was just worried about you."

That made my anxiety worse. "I know. Mac doesn't judge people she cares about. She shouldn't have seen me like that..." The unspoken statement was that I shouldn't have been in that state for her to see me.

It was my fault.

I let out a sigh, making a decision that I should've made months ago.

"I need to find my stuff." Then I'd call Mac, and I'd find her, talk to her. Things were ridiculously distant between us and I couldn't lose Mac.

Cris nodded slowly. "Okay."

"I need to check the back of your truck. My phone might've fallen out of my pocket or something."

He gave me a guarded look before stepping back, his hands falling from my shoulders. "We can check, but we should check Lauren's car." He motioned to her. "She gave us a ride home."

I glanced her way. "You gave us a ride back?"

She nodded, both were studying me so intently, as if reading something that I wasn't aware was on my face. She said, "Yeah, and we can check, but I don't think anything fell out of your pocket. I was looking all over my car this morning for my supplies and I never came across a phone."

"What about keys?"

Her face shuddered. "Nothing that wasn't mine, but we should still check."

There was nothing in the back of Cris' truck. Nothing in Lauren's car either.

"Shit."

Lauren and Cris shared a look before Cris asked, "Where to now?"

I glanced up, seeing both watching me. "My purse is at Troy's place. We can go and see if somehow I left everything inside my purse?"

"Let's go." Cris tossed his keys in the air, catching them as he started back to his vehicle.

Lauren lingered, a hesitant look on her face.

I waited, frowning a little.

"Do you mind if I tag along?"

I shrugged. "Sure. You don't have classes?"

She shook her head. "I was going to spend the entire day in the art studio, but honestly, that can wait. I'm kinda invested now, since I'm the reason any of this is happening."

"What do you mean?"

"I knew Hell Skate was playing at Disco Digs last night. I mentioned it to Mackenzie."

"Oh." But, I shrugged. "I should be thanking you then."

Her eyebrows both went high and her head leaned back an inch. "Wh—huh?"

I gave her a slight grin, but only a slight one because my insides were still in turmoil. "A lot of shit's going on in my head right now, but one thing's obvious. I need to connect with Mac again. I don't like not knowing what's going on with her. I shouldn't have let us fade so much. So, thank you."

She blinked at me, a surprised look on her face. "I—uh—yeah. No problem."

She began to climb into the back of Cris' truck, but I said, "I'll go back there." When Lauren looked like she was going to protest, I added, "I want to check again. Just in case."

As she stood back, letting me climb in first and then to the back, Cris said, "You weren't back there last night. Like, at all."

"I wasn't?"

He shook his head as Lauren got in, shutting her door.

My head fell all the way back against the seat. "Well, shit then."

He studied me again as he started the truck and pulled onto the street after I gave him Troy's address. "You worked up about going to this guy's place, or is it something else?"

I looked out the window, hugging myself, and only lifted up a shoulder in response.

I was worked up about so many things.

Hooking up with Cris again, remembering how it felt to come apart under his touch, and knowing it'd be hard to get that out of my system again.

Or that I couldn't remember the last conversation I had with Mackenzie, or what it was even about.

Or that when we got to Troy's, there was a possibility Jude would be there, and what would that interaction look like? With me showing up with Cris?

The thing I was worried about the least was that I didn't know where my phone was. That struck me as funny for some reason, and my mouth twitched as I tried to hold in my laughter.

Then I couldn't, and once one laugh escaped, another joined it, and a third, and a fourth. Soon I couldn't stop laughing because in all realness, my life was so messed up and I was only now starting to play catch-up.

I was aware of Cris and Lauren's attention on me, but I thought about talking to Mac, reconnecting with her again, and the inevitable question would come up. What happened to us? What happened to me? And I'd have to tell her, because it was Mac and she was the bestest kind of friend there was, and when

I told her—my laughter dwindled—then I'd have to tell Cris too.

The laughter died.

I stopped thinking instead.

# 7

## MACKENZIE

Kellie Rispins was insane. I'd learned that from my online search.

"Babe?"

I stiffened, before remembering that Ryan texted earlier, asking how I was. I'd only told him I was in the library, and it was now in the afternoon. I couldn't make myself leave for my second class of the day.

I looked over, seeing him coming toward me with a frown.

More than a handful of people were checking him out.

Macquire Univeristy was a big college. Lots of students, but Ryan was Ryan Jensen and well, he was treated like a celebrity. He'd gotten that treatment already in high school, and it hadn't changed. It got *more* and because of that, we didn't spend a lot of time out and about on campus. Me being in the library and still being here was probably was not the norm. He came over, sitting down in the chair beside me. A computer was in front of him, but he ignored it. "You were here all day?" He reached over, smoothed a hand down my back as I leaned forward.

I nodded. "I need to tell you something."

His frown deepened, but he was looking me over, heavy concern on his face. "Did you eat?"

I'd been about to tell him about the blogger girl, but asked, "What?"

"Lunch. You didn't eat anything for breakfast. Did you skip lunch too?" He was still taking me in, his eyes tracking over every inch of me, to my bag, to my things spread out around the computer, and lingering on my coffee cup.

Understanding dawned.

Oh, shit. He was worried about me, like worried *worried* about me.

I flinched before reaching for his hand, scooting my chair closer to him. I lowered my voice. "Hey."

His eyes met mine, but he was still searching inside of me, trying to figure out what was going on with me and if it was something deeper he needed to worry about. "Yeah, babe?" His hand cupped the side of my face, holding me in the palm of his hand for a moment.

I closed my eyes, leaning into that hand before I looked back at him. I squeezed his hand. "I'm okay. Okay?"

His eyes clouded. He didn't answer.

Regret hit me low in my sternum, but it only flared briefly. What I went through, what happened to my sister, I knew I'd get this look from him. And I knew in a way that I'd always get this look from him, but guilt spread through me. This was the struggle with my mental health because when I was good, my loved ones may not be. They may not understand the page I was on was clear and clean, and they might need some extra time to adjust. But I also felt bad because he wasn't my father or my brother. I didn't want him to have that constant look of worrying about me, or reading into anything I did out of the ordinary.

But Ryan being Ryan, he wasn't saying anything. He was just trying to silently figure it out.

"Hey." I took his other hand from my face and leaned close, whispering, "I have not lied to you. We have a system, right?"

He nodded. "Yeah."

"When I start struggling, I'm supposed to tell you. And I will. I'll tell you."

He wasn't convinced. The cloudy look hadn't cleared.

I leaned in, my lips meeting his for a soft kiss. "I will tell you. I promise."

"But what if you don't know yourself?"

"I'll know. I promise."

He scanned everything I had spread out around the computer again, the side of his jaw clenching.

"Hey." I touched the side of that square jaw that I loved so much and brought him back to looking at me. "I don't get like this with my stuff. I think Willow did, but that's not me. And I *will* tell you, but this isn't that. I'm good. I promise." I moved my hand, laying it against the side of his face, hoping he can feel that I'm me. I'm not something else.

He nodded, breathing out some air. "Okay. Yeah. I just—" His eyes closed. "I don't want you to ever suffer and I—"

"I know. I do." I moved in, my mouth brushing over his again.

He relaxed, but I started to lean back. He didn't let me, opening his mouth over mine and taking control of it. Ooooh. Deep and dark hunger lit up inside of me, as his mouth now was commanding mine.

*Click.*

He froze first.

*Click, click.*

Tearing his mouth away, he scanned the room and shoved up from his seat. "Are you fucking kidding me?"

It took me longer to realize what was going on. Ryan's kiss had left me in a daze, but I stood up, seeing him approaching a group of girls who had their phones out, pointed at him. A few were still pointed at me.

Oh, no. One was filming this while another was backing up, trying to put her phone away quickly.

The clicking sounds. They'd taken pictures of us kissing.

"Ryan," I said, my voice hoarse.

Gah. I needed to get to him, but I couldn't leave all of this out in the open. They might swoop in and take pictures of this too. "Ryan, stop."

"Dude," a hiss came in from the side as someone was there, getting between Ryan and the girl who was now backed up against a table. She was slightly trembling. "Stop, man."

I had to blink a few times before accepting what I was seeing.

It was Cameron Cahill, a hand to Ryan's shoulder, and he was herding him away, blocking Ryan's view of the girls. He pushed him toward me, looking over my shoulder and seeing I was trying to get all my stuff together and shutting my computer down. His eyes only flicked once to the screen before refocusing on Ryan again.

My chest loosened suddenly. He hadn't really seen anything on the computer.

"What the fuck are you doing?" He was speaking in a low tone, his eyes flashing. His hand gripped Ryan's shoulder tighter, and I wasn't liking seeing how his fingers sank even more into Ryan.

With the last item stuffed in my bag, I zipped it up and swung it onto my back as I stepped in, knocking Cahill's grip loose. I stood in front of Ryan, glaring. "You don't have to handle him like that."

Cahill snorted, sneering at me, shaking his head. "Right. Your boyfriend was about to light into some freshman girls. Like that would've been a good look for the team."

Ryan touched the side of my hip, squeezing me lightly, reassuring me he was okay.

Well, I wasn't now. I seethed right back. "He wouldn't have done shit. They were taking pictures of us kissing and a few were filming the entire interaction. Ryan saw that. He wouldn't have done anything more."

"Well, that shit's now out there, and I'm sure he'll have to convince Coach of this instead of me."

"You made it worse."

"Mac." Ryan fitted himself against my back, his chest lifting in a drawn-out motion before he relaxed again. He was okay, and as he separated, moving to stand in front of me, his hand switching to hold mine behind him, he smirked at Cahill, but his words were for me. "I'm fine. We shouldn't be here anyways."

"No," Cahill said haughty. "You shouldn't be. You're not normal, dude. The rest of us, we can get away with being in the library, sharing a kiss with our girlfriend, but you can't."

Ryan narrowed his eyes, but he didn't respond.

He didn't need to. We all knew what Cahill meant. Even himself, he and Ryan were the two best players on the team, and when Ryan joined, he was forced to share the spotlight, but there were three other players on the court with them. But still, Ryan got the focus. He got the attention. He was an NCAA star player, but even that, he wasn't a normal NCAA star player. He was *more*.

I glanced around, seeing the girls were still there. Their phones remained up and pointed at us.

I tugged on Ryan's hand, stepping away. "Let's go." I cast a furtive look in Cahill's direction. "I have things to tell you."

The two guys were still engaged in a heated scowling stand-off, but when I tugged a second time, Ryan let out, "Fine. Yeah." He went with me. When we cut through the small crowd that had formed, I glanced back over my shoulder.

Cahill still stood there, but his head was down and his hands were balled into fists at his side. He stood alone.

Once we got outside, I opened my mouth to tell Ryan everything that happened, my hand letting go of his.

He shook his head at me. "No," he growled, keeping my hand caught in his, and he switched our direction, taking me in the direction of the food courts. "Whatever you have to say to me, you can tell me over food. You're going to eat." His gaze held mine, as if daring me to go against him, but a grin slipped out.

What was a girl to do in this situation? I laughed slightly before saying, "We ran out of time for food this morning, and I was busy during lunch. I'm not starving myself. I'll happily eat, but I do have things to tell you."

He studied me for another beat before his jaw relaxed and his head lifted. "Good. Just—good. I'm..." He hesitated. "Just as long as you're okay."

That guilt was there again, but it'd take time. He loved me. He cared. He didn't want me to hurt, or be sad, or be how I used to be. Warmth surged up in me, filling me completely, knocking that guilt away. We'd had talks about this, hours and hours, and we'd both do our part.

I stopped us, standing in front of him. "It goes both ways, you know."

His eyes fell to my mouth. His hands went to my hips, just holding me there lightly. His thumb moved under my shirt, rubbing over my skin. "I know."

We both had haunts. They were different, but at times, they weren't that different. What affected him, affected me and vice versa, and in the end, we were in it together.

As if sensing where my thoughts had gone, his eyes softened, and he stepped close, kissing my forehead before his hands fell from my hips. "I just need to know you're okay. Okay? I can't function if you're not. I go crazy."

A warmth tunneled in my chest, taking root in there. "I'm okay, except now—" My stomach growled. "—I'm hungry."

The corner of his mouth curved up. He moved to my side, his arm coming down around my shoulder, and he tucked me into his side. "What do you think I'm doing here? I'm trying to *feed my woman*. Let me take care of you."

I let him take care of me.

Then I told him everything because I was taking care of him too.

# 8

# MAREN

Troy's house was a shitshow. His roommates were in another band, which was how he met Luis, Hell Skate's drummer, and the two started hooking up. That lasted two years and now they're boyfriends, so Troy's was a party house. It was the general go-to place before heading out to whatever gig was happening that night. When we showed up, it was still early in the day. I hoped there wouldn't be a lot of people around, and we got lucky.

I let myself in through the back door, which was the common way to get into the house. And you didn't wait. You knocked once, let yourself in, and called out as you did, "Anyone here?" If anyone tried going to the front door, they were ignored.

Cris snorted, following me inside.

Lauren stayed outside because her phone began ringing when we were walking in.

No one was in the kitchen, but I heard people talking in the living room, and Troy's room was on the other side of the living room. There was only one way to get to it.

"Hey..." I trailed off, not seeing who I'd expected. Some of

Troy's roommates. Some random other stranger, or two. Maybe Luis and Troy themselves. I'd not expected to see Jude on top of Toya, and two guys standing in the corner, their dicks hanging out of their pants, and filming the entire thing.

They saw me with different reactions. One got excited, his dick noticeably rising, while the other's eyes got big and fearful. He put his phone away and began doing up his pants. "Oh. Hey, Maren—"

Jude's head ripped away from Toya, looking my way. "Oh—shit. Maren." He paused, his dick inside of her, but he didn't pull out. "Hey..."

I stood there, not sure how to react to any of this.

Toya was in another world, and she blindly reached for Jude, trying to tug him to keep moving inside of her. She had no idea I was even here.

But then again, would it have mattered?

Jude and I weren't exclusive. We hooked up, and we did it often, but there had been an unspoken agreement to keep it just the two of us. Or so I thought because with how Toya was clambering for him, I wasn't thinking this was the first time they got together. And what were the chances too? On the very day I got with Cris, he also got with Toya? I didn't believe in coincidences.

I shook my head, scoffing. "Thank God I made sure you kept it wrapped with me." But a flat feeling fell in my stomach. I forced myself to start through the living room.

"Hey. Mare—" Jude jackknifed up, his dick now coming out of her, but I wasn't watching him. I shook my head, going past them to Troy's closed door. I knocked as I heard Jude scrambling behind me. The sounds of clothes rustling, a zipper being done up.

"Troy?" I said. "You in there?" I tried the handle. Amber said to go in, and it was unlocked so I began turning the knob.

"Maren. Hey. Can we talk about this?"

I opened the door, stepping in when I didn't see anyone.

Amber said he'd put my purse in the closet, so I crossed the room to that door.

"Maren, seriously." Jude had followed me inside, his jeans undone, but pulled up and hanging low on his lean hips. He had no shirt on, showing off his slightly ripped chest with his tattoos.

I glanced at him, thinking how I used to think he was so hot. The barbell through his eyebrow. How his hair was messily rumpled. But, no. That wasn't totally true. I needed someone to take my mind off of Cris, and Jude had been attractive. He appeased me. It took two months of us hooking up before I started thinking he was hot. I'd spent the summer at his house, sleeping at his side, going to his practices with him, his gigs, generally being his girl in so many ways. Everyone thought we were exclusive.

But after feeling Cris again, after just being around Cris, after waking up in his arms again, there was no appeal for Jude anymore. He'd killed it. And this, him with Toya, it would've been over anyways.

"Can we talk about this?" His voice rose, getting mad. He stood in the doorway, and I felt his gaze on me, his eyes scorching me and not in a good way.

I still ignored him, opening the closet and relief swooshed through me. My purse was tucked in the corner, by the wall. Just where Amber said it would be. I snatched it and went through it, more relief making my knees shake. My phone was in the front pocket, and my keys were in the main part. I took my wallet out, checking, and everything was there.

My God.

I had to sit down.

How had I gotten so lucky?

I needed to send Troy a thank-you basket.

"Listen." Jude had come to the closet door, hitching his

jeans up as they began sliding down. "Can we talk about this? We never said we were exclusive—"

I looked up at him. "What are you talking about?"

"What are *you* talking about? You walk in and I'm fucking Toy—"

"Maren?" Toya screeched from the living room. "Where is she? Where is that bitch?"

That bitch?

Oh hell no.

I grabbed my purse, pushed up to my feet, and started for her, but Jude got in the way. I glared at him. "Get out of my way."

He ran a hand down his chest, some of his panic leaving. A cocky smirk replaced it. "Let's talk about this. She doesn't mean anything."

I shoved past him, all of this starting to grind inside of me.

"Babe." His hands went to my arms. He started to halt me while Toya was still shrieking from the living room until he was ripped away from me.

*Thud.*

He was shoved up against the wall by Cris, his hand to Jude's throat. "You don't fucking put hands on her." A savage growl came from him. A hanging picture fell from the wall as Jude tried to shove back, but Cris only slammed him once again to the wall, holding him in place.

Anger emanated off of him in waves.

Toya began yelling all over again, but Jude was trying to fight back, snarling. "Who the fuck are you—oh! OH! You're the guy she needed—" His eyes went to me over Cris' shoulder. "Really? You're fucking him again? Should I expect you crawling back in my bed in the future? Begging me to 'make me forget him. I need to just forget about him.' Hmm, sweetheart?" A twisted laugh sounded from him as he shook his head. "This is fucking priceless. What are you thinking, Mare Bear?"

"Don't call me that," I warned.

"What the fuck are you talking about?" Cris' tone was flat.

Jude's gaze found his and his laugh just doubled. "This is so fucking priceless. Here I am, having a mild heart attack, thinking I'm going to lose my dick privileges in the ever-so-unquenchable Maren, thinking she'll take offense to my dick being in one of her friend's when the entire reason she sought me out is here. And look at you." He pointedly looked at Cris' arm, where he was still holding him back. "You're here to what? Protect her from me?" He began laughing again. "Please. I don't know what you did the last time, but I've no doubt you'll do it again, and that's when sweet little tortured Mare Bear will come back to me." His gaze switched to me, starting to heat up. A cruel glint showing. "I'll make you beg this next time. I'll make you do nasty things. Maybe we'll take a spin with Toya, hmm? The two of us both pounding her sweet—"

I pressed a hand to my stomach. "You're going to make me vomit."

He snorted. "Right. Was it the thought of both of us tag-teaming Toya together?"

"No," I growled, stepping up to him. "It's the thought of me ever being with you again. You disgust me." Before anyone could stop me, I reached between their bodies, grabbed Jude's dick, and I twisted.

He screamed, his body seizing up.

Cris stepped back, letting him go, but his arm wrapped around me instead. He lifted me away, carrying me back through the living room.

The two guys were still there, but so were a bunch of others. Amber, Troy, and Luis stood in the kitchen doorway. Lauren was right in front of them. Toya was gone, but she began yelling from the bathroom, the door heaved open, and those two guys were there, blocking her way. One twisted around and yanked the door shut again. He yelled through it, "Stay the fuck in there."

"You—" she began yelling again, but it was inaudible.

Another deep *thud* came from behind us, along with Jude still screaming in pain.

Lauren's eyes were big as she looked past us. "What'd you do to him?"

I grunted as Cris swept past her, past them, and carried me all the way outside without stopping. "Hoping I castrated him." The door banged shut behind us before he put me back down on my feet, but he crowded me, not letting me go back inside.

Amber, Luis, Troy, and Lauren followed us out.

Lauren grinned, moving around them, and coming to stand by us. "I snapped a pic of him, and I know those guys in there. They were recording the whole time. Heath said he'd share the video with us if we needed it for some reason."

"You okay, Maren?" Troy came over, his hand going through his blond hair.

I liked Troy. He was the kind one in their whole group, but also tortured at times too. Striking good looks, he modeled at times to pay the bills. Luis was next to him, in a way so opposite his boyfriend. Troy varied between being pale at times, to being sun-kissed tan. Luis had brown skin, thick black eyebrows. Dark black hair. And almond deep eyes. They were both lean, similar height, just under six feet, but Luis had a mean side to him except when it came to Troy. Luis was also a smartass at times too, and there was no love lost between him and Jude, which caused a lot of drama among their band. Still, he slung an arm around Troy's shoulder, and I caught a twinkle of concern in his eyes too.

He repeated Troy's question. "You okay?" Adding with a jerk of his head toward the house, "The others are about done with him. Say the word, I'll make an ultimatum. Me or him." He smirked, leaning against Troy. "We can get another good singer, but great drummers are another thing. They'll kick him to the curb, no problem."

I just gave him a tight grin because my mind was trying to grapple with everything that just happened.

Jude had been fucking Toya. How long had that been happening?

But what Jude said... I eyed Cris warily, because he'd heard. And his eyes were on me, and they were not happy. He was pissed, but his mouth was clamped shut tight. Whatever he was going to say to me, to question me, he was waiting until later.

A shiver went through me, thinking about how that was going to go.

Amber said, "You got your purse." She grinned at me, some stress lines surrounding her mouth. There were heavy bags under her eyes too.

I shot Troy a look and held up my arm. "Thank you for this."

He nodded, flashing me a smile, and relaxing under Luis's arm. "Of course."

I asked Amber, tensing, "How long? Him and Toya?" There was also another question unspoken.

She seemed to deflate in front of me. "He was fooling around with her before you came onto the scene."

I stiffened in shock.

"She told me they stopped, but apparently," she motioned to the house, "you can see they hadn't."

Fuck. Fine. I would have to ask, "Did you know?"

Guilt flared in her gaze before she looked away.

She knew.

She turned away, hugging herself.

Luis and Lauren were both gauging her reaction before Luis snorted, flicking his eyes upwards. "They were hiding it until August. They stopped hiding it after that. You just weren't around as much, so they got away with it."

"You didn't think to tell me?"

He shrugged, not caring. "Bro code, sweetness. Plus, Jude kept telling us you weren't exclusive."

"We weren't, but—"

Troy stepped away from Luis, rounding on him. "Toya was her friend!" He shot me a look. "I didn't know. Swear to you or I would've said something."

I believed him. "Thanks, Troy." My eyes flicked to Luis and I relented, "But he's right. Jude and I weren't ever boyfriend/girlfriend. We just hooked up all the time."

Troy started to say something, but he swallowed his words, his eyes shooting to Cris, who began growling.

I tensed, edging away from him to the side.

"I don't fucking think so." He began to reach for me. "I've been patient, but you and me, we've got shit to discuss. I'm done waiting."

"Cris," I started, then yelled in surprise as he bent down and threw me over his shoulder. "Cris!"

He ignored me, glancing to Lauren. "We're going. You need a ride?"

Her eyes were still big, but she was smiling widely. "Nah. My friend is coming over. She can pick me up. Plus, I think there's going to be fireworks here and I can't wait to watch it. I'll tell you everything."

"Fine." He swung around, going to his truck.

Amber ran after us. "Maren!"

He paused, but just barely.

She rushed out, "I'm sorry. I should've told you about Toya. I—I'm sorry."

I waved her off. "Honestly, I should've expected it."

"You're not mad at me? You still want to be friends?"

"No, Amber."

Her eyes fell.

Cris was on the move again.

She followed as he opened the passenger door, putting me inside. He glanced at her once before scorching me with a warning look. "You fucking leave and I'll—"

"If I were to go anywhere, it wouldn't be to stay here."

He scowled, but moved past Amber, going to his side of the truck.

She gave me a sad smile. "I liked having you here."

I nodded, but didn't say anything else. We both knew the deal. There were reasons she was friends with Toya, reasons she hung out with the band, reasons she liked to get drunk and do drugs to get numb just like me. It just happened that my reason stopped making sense the second I woke up in Cris' bed this morning. I had things to tell him and things to tell Mackenzie.

As Cris got in, his door shut, and he started the engine, he barked, "Shut the door."

I reached for it, pulling it closed.

Amber didn't say anything more, and she didn't wave, but she watched me go, just like I watched her until I couldn't anymore. It was a goodbye in our way, and it was significant for us both.

I said under my breath, though I knew Cris would be able to hear, "Hope you face your demons too one day, Amber."

Cris asked tightly, his jaw clenched, "That's what I am to you? One of your fucking demons that you were trying to run away from?"

I looked his way, feeling a sudden sadness come over me. "No, Cris. You were my Christmas song." I looked away, adding, "Until you broke my heart."

# 9

## MAREN

How did I know he was going to drive us to his house? If I'd been a betting woman, I would've not made anything because I would've been betting with myself, but I was right when Cris wheeled into his parking spot. He was out of the truck, his door slamming shut the next second, and he wasn't waiting. He stormed inside.

A part of me considered calling an Uber, or walking. I could've done with the exercise and I had all my stuff now, but I'd started this. Or, well, Cris did. Or Mac did? Or, no. Lauren did because she's the one who mentioned where Jude's band was playing last night, so Lauren started this. Lauren could finish it.

That made no sense, but I was procrastinating because I already knew what I was going to do and I was terrified.

Reaching for the door, I climbed out and went inside.

Two of his roommates were in the kitchen. Both paused, frowning at me. I held up a hand. "He went to his room?"

One narrowed his eyes at me, a spoon held in front of his mouth. The other one nodded, grunting. "A reminder that we've got practice at three, hmmm?"

"Right," I muttered, shuffling past them and turning the corner, going to the far end. His door was closed, but I opened it.

"What the fuck do you mean I broke your heart?" Cris was glowering, looking all murderous as he'd been waiting for me to show up.

I stepped in, closed the door, and said the reminder, "You have practice at three."

"What?" he barked, then glanced at the clock. "Shit." He pulled his phone out.

"What are you doing?"

"Setting an alarm in case we fuck."

My eyebrows went up. "I thought we were about to fight."

He cast me a look.

I closed my mouth. Right. Fighting might lead to fucking.

When he was done, he tossed his phone on top of his laundry basket where a blanket was folded up. "Christmas song? Broke your heart? I don't understand that. Oh, and what else did that asshole say? That you fucked him so you'd forget about me? *What the fuck,* Maren? Start talking."

Right.

I took a breath, ignored the pain that sliced through my chest, and started. "We started hooking up around Halloween."

"Yeah. So?"

I couldn't look at him when I was going to say all of this, so I went past him, sat on his bed, and turned so I was facing the wall. He shifted around to watch my back, but I could feel his restlessness. He was like a caged tiger that was hungry and got his first scent of food. His energy was assaulting, but I ignored that too. "We just hooked up. It was fun. New. Easy."

"Already knowing all of this shit, Maren."

"We had sex on Thanksgiving. You remember that too?"

He quieted, but said, "Yeah. You and Mackenzie stayed. The

four of us had our own Thanksgiving dinner that night at the dorms." He blew out a ragged breath. "We fucked that night." An abrupt laugh came next. "We fucked like four times that night."

"Yeah." I closed my eyes, my chest stinging. The pain was fresh as I was reliving it all over again. "I fell in love with you on Christmas Eve."

I heard nothing behind me.

I kept going, some numbness starting to seep in, thankfully. "The next day, you were my Christmas song. It's what I listen to, that makes me happy. I usually have one during the holidays because I love Christmas, but it can be a song during any time of the year. You were my Christmas song. You were supposed to make me happy. I wanted to keep you. Forever. I wanted you to tell me you loved me too, and the four of us would be friends forever. Ryan and Mac are endgame, but I wanted you and me to be endgame too."

"Maren," he said so quietly.

My heart shattered all over again because how had he not known? Truly? I hardened myself and stood, looking at him. His face was closed down, but I saw the regret in his eyes. That said everything. I shook my head. "Don't. It's not even anything surprising. Friends with benefits. I knew the deal. I broke the deal. That's on me. Me." Nope. The numbness was sliding away and the pain returned. It was sweltering this time around. I almost pitched forward, just to ease some of it away, as if I could stand in a different position, it would help in some way. That was also foolish, like I'd been back then. "Starting basketball player, as a freshman too." I whistled. "You were the dream, Chavez."

His eyes flared at the use of his last name.

I cocked my head to the side. "You're tall. You're hot. You're amazing in bed. And you liked fucking me. I thought we were on the fast track to falling in love, until I was so wrong. I saw you at a party and I remember the date, because it was like the universe was laughing at me. Valentine's Day. How stupid of me."

He closed his eyes slowly, his head falling back a little. "You told me you were going home that weekend."

Now was where the pain really amped up, feeling like razors were being sliced down my insides, slowly, to draw out the torture. "I did. I drove back. Mac said you were at the Phi Beta party since you guys won that night. I went to find you."

We both fell silent because we both knew what I would've seen that night.

He swore, hanging his head. "You never told me. We never had the exclusive talk."

"I know," I said quietly. "All good points."

"But wait. That was February. We kept hooking up until mid-March."

My chest felt like it was being crushed. "Because of those points. We weren't exclusive, and I couldn't bring myself to talk to you about it. I also couldn't bring myself to stop being with you."

He was remembering things himself, saying, "That's why you insisted I glove up. It was after Valentine's Day. You said—"

"I said I was switching my birth control and wanted to be sure. I lied."

His gaze was so heavy on me. "I never slept with that girl."

"There were two other girls. Two other parties you thought I wasn't going to come to and I did, because I needed to see you do it."

He shook his head, a savage curse falling from him. He raked a brisk hand through hair. "This is fucking bullshit. The first girl, you didn't stick around very long because she kissed me. I shoved her off of me and chewed her fucking ass out because as far as I was concerned, I had a girl."

I frowned. "The other two—"

He took an intimidating step toward me, his eyes blazing. "The second girl was the same fucking girl. You didn't look at her very hard because she tried the same thing again. She tried it with every guy on the team. She's a groupie. And the third girl? I was wasted, out of my mind blitzed. We just almost won fucking March Madness, and I was celebrating but also commiserating at the same time. I thought that chick was you."

I—I couldn't breathe. "What?"

"She looked like you. I thought she was you, and I said your name. She said, 'Yes?'" He pivoted away, a murderous expression on his face. "I thought she was you, but you're right. That one I did fuck. I didn't realize my mistake until the next morning, and then I kicked her to the curb and threatened her that if she didn't steer clear from me, I'd go to the authorities because that bitch fully knew that I thought she was you. I was talking to you the whole time I was fucking her."

I couldn't move. I couldn't talk. I hadn't considered any of those possibilities. "Oh, God." Bitterness laced me. "You were— that girl—" What she did to him. . . "Oh my God, Cris." Horror filled me and I gasped, my hand covering my mouth.

"I'm fine—"

I yelled, "You're not fine! That's assault. That's fucking assault, and you're not fine. If that'd been me? If a guy had done that to me?"

"I would've murdered him."

"Exactly," I clipped out. The need for violence was fast fucking filling me. "What was her name?"

He narrowed his eyes on me. "Why?"

"Her name, Cris. What was her name?"

He began shaking his head. "No. You're not—"

"WHAT WAS HER FUCKING NAME?"

The door swung open, and Ryan stood there, his own need for violence on his face. "Kellie Rispins."

I rocked backwards because I knew that name, but for another reason, one that—I stopped thinking and I was *only* feeling.

Mac moved to see inside, and her eyes went wide at seeing my face.

I began shaking my head. Everything was falling apart in front of me. There were still things to tell Cris. There were things to say to Mac too, but what that bitch did—I needed to hurt her. "Mac," I said.

She shoved past Ryan, rushing at me, and she enfolded me in her arms.

I clung to her. "Did you know?"

"No." She held onto me tighter, rocking me from side to side. "No. I had no idea until just now. Everyone could hear you guys."

My hands balled into fists, pressed behind her back. I lowered my voice so only she could hear me, "I need to hurt her. I need to—"

"I know. Me too, but for a different reason."

"What?"

But Ryan was saying to Cris, "We need to talk about that same girl."

Cris threw him a distracted look, his eyes going right back to me. "What?"

"Cris." Ryan stepped in front of him, blocking his view of me. "Rispins is the blogger."

"Wha—move! I need to see my girl."

I reacted, hearing an unhinged feral tone coming from Cris, and pulled out of Mac's arms, running around Ryan. I hit Cris' chest as he had taken a step around his roommate to find me. We collided in an almost violent way, but his arms wrapped around me, and he hauled me up.

All the bullshit was over.

I'd been so stupid. I should've confronted him. I should've. .
. But no. I pulled out of Cris' arms. "She blackmailed me."

He blinked. "What?"

# 10

## MACKENZIE

**B**lackmail?

I shared a look with Ryan, going over to him as Cris gripped her tighter to him. She closed her eyes, resting her forehead to his chest.

"What do you mean, blackmail, baby?"

God. The name. The way he said it. So tender. He loved her. My eyes were almost bugging out, I was sure, because I was so happy for Maren, but also so terrified. Like I was holding my breath kind of terrified because I wanted her to be happy. She deserved to be happy.

Why wasn't she happy?

She wasn't answering Cris. She was only drawing in deep, shuddering breaths.

Ryan's hand squeezed mine as he whispered in my ear, "You ask."

"Maren," I called her name, but I didn't move from Ryan. For some reason, it was important she was in Cris' arms.

She looked up, such agony in her eyes.

It made me pause because I'd been there. I'd felt that at

times as well. I ached, not wanting anyone to experience that emotion. "What do you mean that she blackmailed you?"

"Last year," Maren rasped out. "I know Kellie. She's from my hometown and she knew something that was happening in my family. She threatened to write it up on her blog, which I wouldn't have cared about, but she said she was going to bring Cris' name into it if I didn't leave him."

He stiffened. "The fuck?"

She cast him a wary look before refocusing on me again. Tears swam in those eyes of hers, but she wouldn't let them fall. Her jaw hardened, pushing the tears away. "That's why I—" She looked up again at him before stepping away from him. "My dad was fired from his job last year, because he was arrested for embezzling from the company where he worked."

Cris didn't reach for her, his hands fisting briefly at his side as his jaw clenched.

"He's in prison and she was going to splash it all over campus, said she could do it. I know how articles like that get attention, how the headline would be written. She'd use your name, make it sound like you're attached to my dad going to prison, and I just didn't want any of that to fall on you."

"That's why you started fucking that asshat?"

She flinched, casting me a look before looking down to the floor.

"She's done it before," Ryan spoke up over my shoulder, one of his arms crossing my chest, holding me against him.

Cris glared our way, but the glare wasn't for any of us.

"What do you mean?" Maren blinked a few times.

"She approached Mac earlier today."

Both Cris and Maren went tense. Maren breathed out, "What? No."

Cris narrowed his eyes at Ryan before looking at me. I saw the unspoken question asking if I was okay, and I gave him a slight nod. Relief flared before he looked back to Cris.

Ryan said, "She's the blogger I told you about."

Cris frowned, confused. "Wait. The one who showed up before practice yesterday?"

I sank into Ryan, feeling his own tension ramping up. He clipped out, "Yeah. Same girl."

"I saw that chick. She's not the same girl."

Maren had her phone out and said, looking at it, "She's changed her looks, but that's her. See." She showed Cris her phone, swiping at the screen and adding, "This is what she used to look like."

At seeing both images, he let out a swift curse. "Fucking bitch. That's her. She's put on weight and changed her hair color, but that's the chick who knew I thought she was you." He stared at Maren for a moment before cutting his eyes our way, the storm that was brewing had some pain. "She knew what she was doing. She was wearing clothes Maren usually wears."

"What?"

He didn't look at Maren, still focusing on Ryan. "She was wearing Maren's perfume. That shit that smells like lilacs. She had her hair done like Maren's last year too."

Maren went pale. She looked as if she'd been physically punched in the face, staggered.

Ryan cursed in my ear before his hand touched my hip, nudging me forward. "Go to her. Take her in my room."

I moved without questioning him. He always knew the right thing to do. He'd taken care of me in the same way. I approached Maren, taking her hand, and said softly, "Let's give them a minute." She didn't move. She was frozen in place.

I met Cris' gaze over her head, both of us knowing she was going to lose it.

I tried to give him a smile, because I wasn't going to let that happen, but he'd gone back to watching his girl as shadows flitted over his face. In a way, I was feeling Maren was the most affected by this and I needed to get in there with her. I needed to get inside, where she could hear me, connect with me, or we might lose her all over again.

"Maren." I tugged on her hand. This time she went with me, walking in a daze as I led her down the hallway, around the kitchen where some of their other roommates were standing, all with different expressions on their face, but judging by the tension in the room, they knew something was going down, something serious.

I kept going, up the stairs and into Ryan's room.

She was still in some sort of shock, so I pulled her to the bathroom and ran some water over a washcloth, using it to wash her face when it was warm.

There was a brief knock on the outside door.

I stepped out of the bathroom as one of Ryan and Cris' roommates stuck his head inside. The others were right behind him. He saw me, his eyes flicking behind me. "We're supposed to be at practice, but called Coach and told him some shit's going down. Was I right to do that? He wants to know what's going on because it's a big fucking deal that we're all missing."

I hesitated before stepping more out and shutting the bathroom door behind me. "I—yeah, some shit's going down, but I think most of you guys could go to practice."

His eyes went back to studying the closed bathroom door. "Right, so here's the real situation. I'm coming to you because I'm about to go see your boy downstairs and we need to know how to handle both Chavez and Jensen?"

He was asking, but also not asking at the same time. I got him.

When Ryan needed to be my emotional foundation, he was perfect. Steady. Stable. Calm. And loving. But I was fine now, and when that happened, that meant Ryan didn't have to be, and well, Ryan had another side to him where he wasn't a guy to mess with. His roommates and his teammates were well aware of that Ryan, and that's what he was actually asking, was more trying to gauge how deep this shit was going to be, and how much I'd be affected because that would then affect Ryan.

I shook my head. "It's a little hiccup with me and Ryan. Most of it's about Maren and Cris."

That's all he needed to know. He clipped his head in a nod, already withdrawing from the room. "Got it. We'll get orders from Jensen downstairs." The other guys heard and were moving away, but he paused, once, looking back at the bathroom. "Whatever's going on, let her know she's not alone. Okay? We're not just a team on the court, you get me?" His eyes flashed. "That means our girls too."

"Thanks. I'll—" The door started to open, so I turned around, saying as I did, "—tell her."

The door opened all the way and Maren stood there, but she wasn't in shock anymore. She was pissed.

"He's not going to do anything about her."

I frowned. "What do you mean?"

"I know what she did to him. You know what she did to him, but he's not going to say it. He won't use that word, but we know. That ain't right. And he's a guy. He's not going to tell anyone. He won't go to any authority to get her in trouble, but she's not going to get away with this."

I was catching up, seeing a wrathful side of my friend and liking it.

*Willow, I'm thinking you would get along with Maren.*

"What are you saying?" I asked.

She raised her chin up. "I don't want to just hurt her. I want to ruin her."

A sensation synced inside of me, a feeling of something clicking into place. In these situations, I wasn't the friend who appealed to rationality. Reason. Nope. I tended to enjoy leaning into where we were a little unhinged. It was more cathartic and a lot more fun.

I smiled. "I'm in."

And I swear that I heard Willow laugh beside me, *No joke, Mac. If I ever killed someone, you're the one I'd call because you'd help bury the body.*

I frowned at that idea, then shrugged. There was some truth in that statement.

My phone began ringing after we were in the car.

Maren said, "It's Ryan, again."

I shook my head. I was the one driving because I was the more stable one at the moment, and we were on our way to pick up Lauren. Maren hadn't wanted to include her, but I was adamant. I said as we were leaving the house and going to my car, "We don't have to involve her where she's helping us do anything, but she has this tendency to know people. She might know someone who could help us out, so I want to just ask her about Rispins, see if she knows her or knows someone who knows her."

Maren had been doubtful, but after a quick call, it turned out that I was right.

Lauren did know Kellie and she did not have a high opinion of her. Hence, we were on our way to find Lauren, because from my internet search earlier today, we had enough to blast Kellie on social media. We could put out there what she'd done in the past and what she tried to do, and maybe it might hurt her, but it wasn't enough. If we put out details, it could backfire and get her more attention, so I wanted to find more dirt on her, dirt that we couldn't find online.

We just hung up with Lauren when Ryan's first call came through.

Maren declined his call, but my phone lit up almost immediately after. She sighed, accepting his eighth call, saying warily, "Hi, Ryan."

He was quiet a moment before growling, "Where the fuck is my girlfriend?"

"I'm here. I'm driving."

Maren added quickly, "You're on speakerphone."

"Take me off speakerphone," he ordered briskly.

"No," I called out. "I'm driving."

"Where are you driving to?"

He was trying to rein in some control. There was a threat against us, against me, Maren, Cris, or him, it didn't quite matter to Ryan. It was a threat and I was involved, so his instincts were to find me, claim me, and protect me at all cost. He didn't realize that this time, it was my job to do that for him. Mine and Maren's job. I said, "We're on our way to pick up Lauren."

"Lauren?"

"Yeah. From last night. She's—"

"I know who she is, but why? We're in the middle of something here and I get done talking with the guys and with Coach, and see you both hightailing your asses to your car. What are you doing, Mac?"

I grimaced because he asked me a direct question and I couldn't lie to him. Fuckity fuck fuck fuck.

As if knowing my dilemma, Maren took over, lifting the phone back to her, "We're doing a girls' night."

I shot her a frown, my eyebrows raised.

She mouthed back, "I don't know."

Ryan scoffed into the phone, "You're doing what?"

She quickly added, "Yeah. Um—you guys have practice, so you guys go and do that. Practice. And afterwards, we'll—afterwards, we'll reconvene."

I mouthed at the same time, the same word with the start of a laugh in my throat as Ryan said sharply, "Reconvene?" He added right after, "What the fuck are you guys doing? Mac?" He growled my name.

I was back to flinching because I was going to fold. I'd have to fold, tell him everything, but seeing that, Maren almost shouted into the phone, "Uh—uh—we gotta go. I'm claiming my roommate for the night. You guys do your thing and we'll talk later. Okay? Bye." She ended the call, heaving out a breath. "No offense, but your boyfriend can seriously be intimidat—" She squealed because the phone began ringing again, his name on my screen. She paled, denying the call, and practically threw my phone back at me. "You need to turn that phone off, and I need to correct myself. Ryan Jensen can be seriously scary. I do not ever want to go against him. I'm just stating that, just because."

I shot her a grin. "Like your boyfriend's any less scary? Cris can hold his own. There's a reason those two get along so well."

"That and because they were roommates last year."

We shared a grin, though it was a little shaky for both of us because as I turned my phone off, Maren's phone started ringing. She looked at it and sighed, showing me the screen.

*Hook-up, not a boyfriend calling.*

I barked out a laugh. "You know that's not true, right?"

She shut her phone off too. "What?"

"That he's not your boyfriend. He very much is, you just weren't aware of it. He loves you."

She stilled, hearing my words, before she shook herself out of some sort of reverie. "No. No. He likes hooking up, and he cares. That's it."

I glanced her way.

She turned to look out the window, but she tucked her hand under her arm, both were shaking.

I wasn't sure what to do—if I should push this or let it go?

*Let it go, sister,* Willow spoke up. *They'll deal with that later, but for now, you got one mission.*

She was right.

I thought it at the same time my sister said it to me, *Destroy the bitch.*

# 11

# RYAN

C ris and I were late to practice, but everyone was still in the locker room.

We shared a look because that made no sense since we were almost an hour late. Cahill glared at me as we walked past, and I got two more steps before Coach's door opened. "Jensen, get in here." He shut it, going back to his desk.

Chavez glanced my way, taking my bag with him.

I sent Cahill another look, to see if he knew what I'd be walking into or not. When the other guys came to Cris' room, we gave them a brief rundown that some stuff was happening, but we hadn't given too much detail. Enough where Coach wouldn't filet our asses for being late, but since it looked like the practice hadn't even started—I had no idea what to think.

I knocked on the door, opening it. "Coach?"

He didn't look up from his desk, reading a piece of paper, and gestured to one of the chairs across from his desk. "Have a seat."

I did.

He kept reading, making me wait a few minutes before he

made a disgruntled sound, pushing the paper away. Looking at me, he leaned back in his chair. "What the fuck is going on? I was told about some press outside my goddamn practice yesterday, and now I'm getting a report that a reporter is going to publish an article, saying your girlfriend threatened her today. I was asked if I had a comment on it. Since you're the common denominator, what the fuck is going on? Did you suddenly turn press-hungry over the summer? And more importantly, how much is this going to fuck up my day?"

"Wha—she's going to say that Mackenzie threatened her?" I was half-tempted to look at the floor because my fucking jaw was down there, somewhere. "Are you shi— this is news to me, Coach."

His eyes narrowed. "Let's tackle the first issue. I thought the media yesterday was overkill. Did you ask them to come?"

"No!" I snapped, surging forward in my seat.

He waved me back, unaffected by my outburst, relief crossing his face. "I didn't think so. Now what's this deal about your girlfriend? From what I know about your girl, she's the opposite of someone who'd threaten another person."

Uh, actually. . . I didn't go that wavelength. "This is a blogger, Coach. And she waited outside of Mac's class today, getting in her face and asking about Mackenzie's health and if it's affecting me. Apparently, she was told by some assface source that my playing is being affected by my girlfriend. Which is total fuc—bulshi—crap. It's total crap, if for any reason that yesterday was our first day of practice."

He didn't respond right away, studying me before commenting, "And yet, it's our second day of practice and you're a no-show, and I'm told by your roommates that it has to do with your girlfriend. So, in a way, the source was credible."

That burned. "Except that's what the blogger asked me before our practice yesterday as well."

His head snapped to the side. "You want to run that by me again?"

I did and waited. Our head coach was a hothead, but he was fair and he did not tolerate bullshit, under any circumstances. Chavez told me that I needed to tell Coach yesterday about the blogger's question, but it'd been day one of practice. I wanted a day, one fucking day, to just play ball.

Coach coughed, looking awkward, before he asked, gentling his tone, "*Is* there something going on with your girlfriend? Something that I do need to know about?"

*Fuck no.* I flared up again, but only said, tightly, "No, sir. Mackenzie is fine."

He continued watching me intently, gauging my response before he gave a nod, his shoulders loosening up. "What else do I need to know about, Jensen?"

I narrowed my eyes. "Coach?"

He rolled his eyes, hit the desk with his hand, and made a 'come on' motion with that same hand. "Let's hear it. I got to know you pretty well last year. You play ball and you have no patience for bullshit. It's part of the reason why I like you, but I also know you keep so much shit to yourself that I could probably find an entire mountain of shit I need to know about that I'd never be told. It's normal, somewhat, but you take it to the extreme. Is this blogger going to be a problem? Tell it to me straight."

Fuck. When he said it like that. . . "Yeah, she's psychotic. She blackmailed Cris' girlfriend last year to break up with him while she turned around—" Goddamn! Shit. I'd been about to tell him, and it wasn't mine to tell. I clamped my mouth shut.

"Fuck's sakes." He stood up, went to the door, and hollered, "Chavez. Get your ass in here."

I started to stand up, but as he went back to his desk, he pointed at me. "You stay put. Your ass isn't going anywhere."

He sat and Chavez stepped into the room. "Coach?"

He regarded both of us, almost glowering before he motioned to Cris. "Come in. Shut the door. Sit down." And as Cris did, he added, "You both are going to tell me goddamn everything, and if you don't, if I even think you're holding something back, you'll be running the bleachers for the next practice, and at the end, if you don't do a suicide in under twenty seconds, you're running the bleachers for the next practice. You got me?"

I winced.

"Yes, Coach."

"Jensen? You copy? You got a problem with how I condition my players?"

I shook my head. "No, Coach. And yes, Coach. Understood."

Cris stared at me, hard, before something flashed in his eyes. He held up a finger. "Coach?"

"What? Does this have to do with whatever the fucking mess you got us into with this blogger, or you got a problem with running the bleachers?"

"Neither."

Coach's eyebrows pulled low, but he didn't respond.

Cris cleared his throat. "Just a request to maybe call them shuttle runs instead of suicide drills?"

We both waited, seeing how Coach would react to that.

It wasn't anything typical in our world. We didn't get to be sensitive or complain. We were basketball players, and this was how we were trained. We got yelled at and cursed at, but Coach made us into better basketball players at the end of the day. This was his house. We were just guests in it.

But Coach gave it a thought before giving an abrupt nod, clearing his throat. His eyes shot my way for a split second. "Yes. We'll be making that change from now on."

My nerves combusted inside of me.

Cris sat up taller, affected as well.

Then Coach yelled, "Now fucking tell me what's going on with this damn blogger reporter person."

## 12

# MACKENZIE

I pulled up to a house, and as soon as I did, Maren said, "Oh, thank God."

"What?" I was distracted, because as soon as my car stopped, the back door of the house burst open and a bunch of people streamed outside. Lauren was with them, but she was in the back. Two guys led the charge, an intensity on their faces that I couldn't quite place if it was a good intensity or if I needed to grab Lauren and throw this car in reverse.

I was torn to do both, and *that* didn't make sense.

"Maren." Both guys went to Maren's door. As she opened it, they pulled it wider. The blond one threw his arms around her, tucking his head into her neck. "Oh, Maren." The other guy, who had some gorgeous dark hair, eyed both of them hungrily, tossed his cigarette to the pavement, and joined in the hug. Two other girls went to that side, but stood back, waiting for their hug to end.

Lauren came over to me, jerking her chin up, her hands in her front pockets. "Girl." That was her greeting.

I laughed shortly as I closed the door, watching the group

84 TIJAN

on the other side of my car. I stepped back next to Lauren, saying under my breath, "I'm thinking I missed some things."

She snorted, grinning my way. "Short version highlights is that the dark-haired guy is Luis. Drummer. Kind of a smartass, but also, he's usually right, so keep that in mind. He's fucking the blond guy, who's got a heart of gold and genuinely likes Maren. Everyone's up in arms because they like Maren more than Jude."

"Jude, her ex?"

She nodded. "Maren and Hot Boy Chavez were here earlier, caught Jude fucking another chick, who got the boot as well. So now Amber, the redhead who looks twenty-six, hasn't lost her place in the group, but she lost her other girl hangout toy, Toya. Who, by the way, was the other chick we saw with Maren at the bar last night."

Whoa.

My head was spinning because that was only last night? All of this had happened in one day?

But Lauren was still going. "When Maren left, Troy and Luis had a 'come to Jesus' moment and went inside, declaring they were kicking them both out of their friend group. Then my friend showed up." Her eyes flitted to the other girl, who was slim with smooth brown skin, hazel eyes, and hair that had a reddish tint to it. It fell past the middle of her back, a gentle curl to it with a couple sections in small braids.

Lauren grinned my way. "I *like* her, like her, in case you were wondering. Her name's Manana."

"Is she the one obsessed with Hell Skate?" I remembered Lauren telling me that.

She nodded. "She's friends with Troy too, which is how I know these guys, but the other recent change is that Manana is now Hell Skate's lead singer. Though, they'll probably have to change their name since Jude threw a fit about it, saying he gave the band that name. It was his name. Etcetera etcetera.

And then you called, asking me about Rispins, who I do know, but not that well, but Troy, he really knows Rispins. Also," she leaned close to me, her grin widening, "he hates her with a passion. You wanted dirt on her? He's got it for you."

This was good news, so very good news.

Lauren was reading my face and chuckled. "That's what I'm thinking too. Are you going to tell me why you want to dig up information on this girl?"

I hesitated.

Lauren saw and moved back a step. "Not a problem. No worries." But I felt her withdrawal.

"No." I stopped her, touching her arm. "It's not that. I need to pick my words because some of it's not mine to tell." She looked across the car, and I added, "Or Maren's."

"Oh." Her eyes filled with concern. "Well, whatever it is, Troy wants in and he wants in like I've never seen him. He's the nice one, but when I mentioned her name, I saw a different side to him. He needs to be in on this."

"We'll give the cliffs notes version to the group."

"Okay, but then you need to send Amber packing. I don't trust her."

"Noted."

But when we got inside, Troy marched into the living room and kicked a couple guys that were playing video games out. Once the door closed behind them, he said to Amber, "You too."

Her eyes got big, and for a moment, I thought she was going to argue, but Luis grunted, adding, "Fucking piss off."

Her face tightened, getting red.

He went over to her and leaned down so he was in her face. "You want to keep hanging out with us? You leave now and don't say one word to anyone about any of this. You got me?"

She'd gone pale, but was nodding.

"I hear one word of this slipped, and I don't care if it's you,

I'll be blaming you and you're out of here. Exiled from all band events. You got me?"

She gulped, her eyes darting to Maren, whose face had closed down when we went inside.

"Good. Now get the fuck out." He stepped back, watching her coolly as she literally turned and left.

Once the door closed again, this time behind her, he cursed under his breath and swung back to face the group. His eyes went to me, narrowing, before swinging to Maren and then to the other guy, Troy. When they hit him, they softened dramatically. "Okay. Carry on. You need someone to be the asshole, I got you covered."

"Oh, baby." Troy was melting.

Luis rolled his eyes, but the corner of his mouth lifted up in a grin as he leaned in, kissing Troy and running a hand down his side. "I'll be here, but not at the same time. Carry on." He headed to a back bedroom, closing the door. We heard drumsticks tapping a moment later.

We got started after that, or more specifically, Troy got us beverages, made sure we were all comfortable, and then he spilled the tea.

Also, it was some *very* lovely tea.

## 13

## MAREN

As plans went, it wasn't the best. I had to admit, but under short notice, it was the most solid one we could come up with other than me doing something that would put me in jail. Which I was okay with, if it came down to that. But we were going to try this way first, and the first part of this plan was me approaching Kellie, one on one.

I knocked on her dorm room and then prayed.

It took a bit before she answered, opening the door an inch and staring at me with suspicion. "What are you doing here?"

I huffed, bugging my eyes out at her. "Let me in. I need to talk to you about something."

She blackmailed me last spring. That was months ago, and it had worked. I did what she wanted and no one knew better, until recently. She wouldn't have known that Mackenzie came to find me a day ago, or that we recently reconnected.

We were banking on that.

"Why?"

"Come on! I need your help, okay?" I mixed in the right amount of pleading and desperation while jerking my gaze away because I had some pride too.

That was the image I needed to sell, and fuck me, but I was going to win an Oscar by the end of this night.

I sniffled, balling my hand into a fist before tucking it in my pocket, and I jerked my gaze back to hers, just in time for her to note everything. Her gaze lingered on where my hand was, and it was working. It had to work. I swallowed a knot and rasped out, "Come on. Please. I need your help with something."

"With what?" She still wasn't budging, but the door opened another inch.

She was starting to relent. She was starting to buy the act.

"I need you to—" I looked around, shuffling closer. "What you did to me last year, I need you to tell me how to do that."

I was expecting her to slam the door in my face, but all she did was move back, standing straight. "Why?"

I let out a growl. "Because I found my boyfriend fucking someone else. I walked in and Jude was railing a friend, someone I thought was a friend." And now, I cast aside my acting skills and let my own disdain shine through, the one I felt for her. "I want to ruin the bitch and I want you to tell me how to do it."

She was looking, but I let her see.

I let her see it all.

I wanted to hurt her.

I wanted to destroy her.

She was the one I wanted to ruin, and when she felt I was genuine, she pushed open the door. "Come in."

# 14

# MACKENZIE

We had a camera set up from Maren's bag, with audible. When she went inside, she moved it around, showing the room, and on the counter was what we needed to see.

*"Why do you want to hurt Kellie Rispins so much?"* I asked Troy.

*He drew in a tight breath. "Why? Because she tried to blackmail me because she wanted something from Luis and his band."*

*"Shocker,"* Maren griped.

*He shared a look with her. "She wanted them to let her tour with them this last summer. That one month."*

*Maren had gone still. "She wanted to do what?"*

*"As you know, I got out of that." But he swallowed, grimacing.*

*Dread took root in me. My mouth dried up as I asked, "How'd you do that?"*

*"I have these." He pulled out a baggie of two blue pills. "I gave these to her instead."*

*"What are they?"*

*"Let's just say rich housewives all over the country enjoy these little pills. The high is euphoric and it lasts for days, but it's the strongest in the first five hours. And it helps them lose weight. Kellie*

Bitchins loves these." He grinned then, a slow, calculating one and picked up his phone, sending off a text.

"What'd you just do?" Maren barked.

"I just sent Kellie a text saying I owe her some happy pills. You want to get her talking? You do three things in a row. One, you wait until she's gotten one of these in her system. Wait three to four hours. Then, you show up and you act defeated. Like you need her help. Like you're desperate for her help. She's going to already be high from one of these, and then you show up? A mark that she destroyed? One that she got away with whatever she did to you?"

Maren tensed. "How did you—"

"It's written all over you. If I'd known before I met you, I would've helped you destroy her long before now, but I didn't know." His eyes cast my way. "I now know how you are pre-Jude, if you get what I mean. I'm sorry for whatever she did to you, but you're right. She needs to be stopped."

I spoke up, "What's the third thing she needs to do? You said three things. The pill. Maren showing up and asking for her help. What's the third?"

"She needs to kiss her ass, and I mean really kiss her ass. Lay it on thick. She's a narcissist, and with all three things happening, she's going to want to boast and brag, and Maren's going to give her the perfect opportunity to sing like a fucking canary."

"What about the pill, though? Won't it look suspicious when you suddenly reach out to give her some?"

He stood up, sliding the baggie into his pocket. "No, because for the last two months, I've only given them when I needed something from her. She'll expect me to show up in a few days and ask for a favor from her."

I stood too. "What kind of favor?"

He paused, studying me. "The kind where she was trying to blackmail another friend of mine and I asked her to leave him alone. That kind. I don't sell these. I get these from my doctor, but that doesn't mean I take them myself. I'm not stupid. I don't want to get *fucked up. Kellie Rispins? I have no problem letting her get fucked up. Since she started taking these, I've seen her slowly start to go off the rails, but she's going too slow, and if she hurt Maren? She deserves everything coming her way. Now, excuse me. I need to get these to her so we don't have to wait until midnight to pump her for information."*

The baggie was there, and it was opened, and one pill was gone.

Maren began the rest.

"I need you to tell me how you did it. What you did to me."

Kellie was quiet for a moment until she asked, "You're still roommates with that one girl, right?"

"Mac? Yeah. I never talk to her. After you blackmailed me last year I did what you wanted. I dropped Cris, but that also meant dropping Mac too. It was too hard being friends with her when she's still so tight with Cris. Why do you want to know?"

"No reason..." She almost sang it, sitting down and getting comfortable. Troy was right. She was high from that pill. She was gleeful.

Maren snapped, sounding impatient and desperate. "Are you going to help or not?"

"What do I get out of this? I don't help out of the goodness of my heart."

Maren shrugged, the bag moving up with her shoulder and falling back down. "I don't know. What do you want? I can't dump Cris again."

"I never told you to—"

Maren jerked forward a step. "Cut the bullshit. You did too. My dad went to prison and you told me, very bluntly—what were the exact words? 'Dump your boyfriend and I won't publish my post linking his name to what your dad's going to prison for.' I hated you. *Hated* you, but I know how you are and what you can do. You could've really hurt Cris somehow, just insinuating a connection. I did what you wanted and I need to know how to do that. What do you want for your help this time?"

"I want access to your roommate's computer."

I stiffened. *My computer?*

"What?" Maren moved back a step. "Why—"

"Do you want my help or not?"

"I do, but—"

"No buts." Kellie surged to her feet. "You either get me into your roommate's computer or I don't help you. That's it. That's the deal. It's your choice."

There was no sound. Kellie was watching Maren, eyeing her until she growled. "Fine! But—"

"But nothing."

"I said *fine*. Okay? You help me first because after what you made me do last year, there's no way I'm letting you burn me again. You help me first and *then* I'll get you into Mac's computer."

"If you don't..."

"You blackmailed me." Maren cut out briskly. "My father went to prison. You knew my family was struggling. My little sister overdosed, and you told me that if I didn't end things with Cris Chavez, you'd post everything going on in my life for everyone to read and you'd insinuate in some way that Cris was involved. You told me flat out that you would ruin his life as well as mine, and you had no problem doing that. I am not stupid. If I don't follow through, you're vindictive enough to come after me again. *So fucking* tell me how to ruin this girl's life because that's what you do, isn't it? You ruin people's lives and you get off on that shit."

Both went quiet. I couldn't see Maren's face, but I heard her harsh breathing. Kellie's eyes narrowed, and she was glaring at Maren. They were in a standoff, but then as if coming to a decision, Kellie shook off the glower and a very slow, very cruel smile appeared again.

She sat back down and crossed her legs. "This is what you do."

She told her.

I sat there, stunned, because she was laying everything out there.

How to get information on her target.

How to find her target's weaknesses.

How to analyze which angle to take for the maximum effect with the least amount of exposure.

She was happy to spill, and the longer she spoke, the more she said, and the faster she spelled it out. Troy was right. She wanted to boast. She was getting off on it all over again.

Maren and I listened to her talk for two hours.

Two complete hours we sat there and just let her tell us who she was.

After she slowed down, she blinked a few times, as if coming out of a trance. "Is that enough? Does that help you?"

Maren didn't move. I didn't know if she could, because I was feeling the same thing, but Maren coughed. "Uh, yeah."

That was my cue.

I left my car and began heading into Kellie's apartment building. We'd already talked about the plan to get inside in case I would need to be buzzed in, but at that moment, a couple guys walked outside so I caught the door and slipped inside easily.

It was meant to be.

"Listen," Maren's voice went somber.

I checked the monitor and she had moved closer to the door, which had been our plan. If I couldn't have gotten in, I was going to buzz her apartment. Maren would've let me in, and if Kellie had questioned her, she would've acted impatient, saying something like, "I don't know who that was. A fucking pizza delivery person. Who cares? They won't bug us again." And she would go right into the next segment.

This time, I paused just coming up to the third floor where Kellie lived because I knew Maren was about to go real. I heard her say, "I need to know what you're going to do when you get into Mac's computer."

I stilled, in mid-step and waited, my heart starting to pound.

I watched the monitor.

Kellie started to roll her eyes, a dramatic sigh coming from her.

Maren snapped, "She's been my only friend here."

"She's not your friend. Like I haven't watched you? Like I haven't watched her? You've barely seen her since starting school this year. The two of you are not friends. Not anymore. And she's weak."

Pain sliced me.

"You don't want someone like her as your friend. She's nothing but weak. Crying. Saying how sad she is. I did you a favor, cutting someone like that out of your life."

*Oh, this bitch.*

Willow was *not* happy.

I almost snorted, because she had no idea. She truly had no fucking idea.

*I'm going to enjoy enlightening her, Sis.*

I started forward again, and as I did, Willow didn't respond.

Kellie was going to learn how very wrong she was, and I was so going to love that I would be the cause of her fall. It was such sweet karma.

And I approached her door, hearing their voices as a low murmur through it, my own sense of euphoria began to spread through me. It was as if the universe was on my side, helping me.

Maren finally broke out, her voice strained, "I'm going to do it, but I just need to know why? What are you going to do?"

Kellie yelled, "What do you think I'm going to do? I get in there and I'm sure she'll be like most people. Her passwords will probably be automatically saved and I can get into any program of hers I want to. Her social media. Her email. I know who her therapist is and I know that there's a program her therapist had coded. It's an online journal where she can get access to what her clients read. Again, what do you think I'm going to do with your roommate? I'm going to find all her dirty little secrets."

Maren got quiet, real quiet, eerily quiet. "You're going to blackmail her?"

"I'm not going to make her break up with her boyfriend, if that's what you're thinking. That's a lost cause with those two, and besides, I was really only into—" She shut up before clearing her throat. "Fine. You want to know what I'm going to do? Really want to know? I'm going to turn every Macquire University fan against Ryan Jensen's girlfriend. I'm going to twist reality and confound every single one of them until they blame her for any mistake he makes. Any game they lose, they'll blame her. Every foul he makes. Every rebound he misses. Every time the ball misses the net, whether it's from him or his teammates, they're going to blame her. And this is going to keep happening until I shatter her, and when that worthless mentally defective piece of trash breaks apart, it's going to destroy Ryan Jensen. And that's what I really want. I want Jensen broken. I want him to lose his mind because everyone will know why her sister ki—"

I was just outside their door, and hearing every word, ice formed over my organs.

Every single one of them.

This girl. She had no idea. No idea how wrong she was, but she would, and she would very shortly.

Maren ground out, her voice hitching because she was on the verge of losing her control, "This is about basketball?"

"No." Kellie heaved out a dramatic sigh. "None of this is about basketball."

"Why then? For views on your blog?"

"God no. I'm doing this as a gift for Cahill."

The fuck?

"Cahill?" Maren burst out.

"Yes. Cameron hates Jensen. The fans might not have realized how much he hates him, but I'm a journalist. We hear all the behind the scenes information. All the gossip. Cahill's been after Jensen since he got here last year, but he wasn't thinking of the big picture. He was only trying to ice him out from the team. He wants Jensen gone and Jensen's weakness is his girlfriend. That's why I'm going to destroy her. And then I'm going to tell Cameron how I gift-wrapped his future basketball career for him, handing it over to him on a silver platter, by getting Ryan Jensen out of his way. And the best part of all of this is that no one will have any idea that the tragic events that will happen to Ryan Jensen and his girlfriend were masterminded by someone else." I didn't need to see the monitor to know the smug smirk she would be wearing. It oozed through her voice. "By me."

She sounded victorious already. She was so sure everything was going to happen exactly how she wanted it to happen, and the sad part was that in the past, it *had* happened how she wanted it to happen.

She hurt other people and she got away with it.

I started to reach for the door handle. It was almost my turn, my entrance.

Maren said, her voice dropping low, "I never would've taken you for a pill popper."

I waited.

Kellie laughed. "What?"

"That blue pill over there. I saw that same bag earlier today, except there was a second pill with it. That's a seriously strong antipsychotic medication. Do you have—"

"No! Shut up."

There. Right there.

That was the first break for us. Kellie just broke, just a little bit.

"That has nothing to do with you," she kept on, some panic rising in her voice. "I helped you out and told you exactly how to destroy this girl's life. Now it's your turn. I want into your roommate's computer. I'll come over to your dorm tomorrow and—"

"You know what, Kel?" Maren bit out, letting her resentment slip through.

It was my turn.

Maren was saying as she opened the door, "I figure let's ask the source herself."

And there the fuck I was.

I smiled, stepping into the room.

Blood drained from Kellie's face.

I held up my phone, letting her see the screen, and I hit end before sending the entire video to Troy.

"Wha—what are you doing here? What was on your phone?"

I said, "Thanks for all of that."

She swallowed, her eyes jerking between Maren and me. "What are you up to?" Her face grew dark, anger filling it. "If you even think of fucking with me—"

I held up my hand, stopping her. "One second, please."

Maren burst out laughing.

I was watching my phone, waiting to get the alert from Troy, and a moment later, it came through. I turned my attention back to Kellie and smiled widely again. "They were already hearing everything, but I needed to send them the file so they could pull what they needed from it."

"What?" Reality was starting to set in, and she stumbled back a step. Her voice was hoarse.

"Yeah." I took another step toward her, dropping my voice

too. But I sounded hard instead. Unrelenting. "We needed audio bites for the article."

"Article? What article?" She wasn't even looking at Maren. She was only focused on me.

*Get her, Sis. Let her see who you really are.*

I didn't need extra encouragement from Willow, but it was appreciated.

I told her, "The one that is going live as soon as they upload all those things you just admitted to doing and are planning on doing. You say you're a journalist, but you're not. What you do, hurting me to hurt Ryan for Cahill. Getting that one girl to hurt herself until she ended up in the hospital? Getting that one guy to drop out of school because you wanted his job in the admissions office? Trying to blackmail Troy? Actually blackmailing Maren to end things with Cris so you could instead dress up like her when he's wasted out of his mind and fuck him." She paled all over again, her eyes jerking to Maren. I moved in front of her, not wanting her to see any pain there because she didn't deserve to see it.

I kept on, "We have other examples. I found them earlier today when I did a deep dive online about you. I saw a pattern, that you go after people's significant others to make them do what you want and you don't care who you hurt."

An alert sounded on my phone, and I pulled it up, seeing Troy had shared the article with me.

I held it up, showing her. "Now the whole world, or let's be honest, the world that cares about this college and our star basketball players will know about you, about Maren, about Troy, about what you were going to do to me. We left Cris out because that's his decision, not ours. They're going to know what kind of person you are. And while I'm hoping that this article gets traction and attention, and that anyone in authority over you will deem it necessary to punish you, or at the very least, prevent you from hurting more people, I also am aware that I can't rely on any of that happening. So instead, this will be out there forever. If you get this taken down somehow, we'll put it up somewhere else. And again. And again. Until you finally stop trying to get it taken down and you will live with it out there. Because everyone has dreams. Including yours. And I want to be a part of the effort to take that dream away from you. One day, when you're hoping to get hired as a journalist, your potential employers will do their own deep dive on you. They'll find this article and will see how you operate to get your stories. No one will hire you. No media source will want you on their team because you're a liability. You're too damaging for them. This article will never go away."

I took another step closer, dropping my voice so it was almost soft. "How do you like that, Kellie? Having one of your darkest secrets out there on the internet for anyone to find? Sucks, doesn't it? Makes you feel violated, doesn't it?"

I heard Maren opening the door behind me and knew it was time to leave.

She saw what we had on her. She saw what we did with it. Now it was time to let the article do the rest.

I leaned in because I had one more thing to say. "You messed up with me. I was your mistake. How does that feel? That this mentally defective weak-minded person is actually the one who fought back first. And want to know why that is? Because I'm *not* weak-minded. Because I'm *not* mentally defective. The shit I've gone through would bring you to your knees in one day. You think about that." And because I saw an ominous gleam flash in her eyes, I didn't need a guess to know what that look meant.

"Mac." Maren prompted me.

It was time to go. I knew, but I had one more thing to say, one more weapon to take away from Kellie. "You want to threaten me? That you're going to tell the world that my twin sister killed herself and she used my suicide note when she did it?"

Maren gasped behind me.

She didn't know that part.

I paused, but a surge of support blasted me from somewhere.

Maybe the universe?

Willow?

Or just myself.

I didn't need it. I was standing just fine on my own as I finished it.

"No need." I held the phone back up, showing the article. "I already did that for you."

# 15

## MAREN
### LATER.

Mac sat on the edge of her bed, her hands tucked under her legs. Her shoulders slightly hunched, but just barely and she watched me. She wasn't hiding. She wasn't shifting. She was waiting. Calm.

"I had no idea." And I had no idea what to say, how to say whatever I needed to say. I knew about Mac's sister, but not... I couldn't even finish that thought.

"I had no idea about your dad. Or your sister. I'm so sorry, Maren."

My throat swelled up, closing.

It'd been the worst time in my life. Had been. I waved her off. "I'm not trying to brush it under the rug, but I'm okay. My family's okay. My dad, he did what he did. He's in prison, but it's not one for hardened criminals. And my sister, she went to rehab. She's actually doing really well. My mom was struggling for a while, until my sister overdosed. After that, it gave her purpose. The two of them are tight. They're in counseling together. They go to a gym five days a week. They're thinking about doing motivational talks. Again, I'm not trying to downplay it, but my family is okay now. We'll be okay."

God. I couldn't get it out of my head.

Mac's words.

" . . . *you're going to tell the world that my twin sister killed herself and she used my suicide note when she did it?*"

"Mac." I couldn't. Her name came out as a whimper. A tear slipped down my cheek.

I wouldn't have gotten through last year if it hadn't been for Mac, knowing she was here, that I had already met her, knowing I would come back to her because that had been the plan in the back of my head. The whole time. I knew she was there. She was constant. I had relied on her being there, and hearing that, it broke a part of me.

Her shoulders lifted up as she drew in some air, then she gave me such a sad smile. Her head tilted down and she shrugged one shoulder, just one, and it was such a small move-ment. "I got sad at the end of last year. I didn't notice at first. You weren't around. Ryan was busy. He had a lot of meetings about summer training, and we went home. My brother was at his school. I know I've told you about him, but he's a little genius. He's at his genius camp year-round, or that's how he describes his school." She rolled her eyes, scoffing, but I heard the pride in her voice. "He does that to downplay it because the truth is that my brother is a genius, and whoever he becomes, he's going to be someone great. I just know it. My parents were there, but they were busy. It wasn't that I was alone. It was just that. . . It snuck up on me and I hadn't looked for the red flags. Then, Ryan found me and he freaked out."

"He found you? What do you mean he found you?" Had she. . . God. I couldn't even let myself think it. Like if I did, it'd come true.

I didn't understand this stuff.

I didn't want to understand it.

"It was our birthday when Willow killed herself. I found her. And it was on the anniversary of that day when Ryan found me. I wasn't in any bad way. I don't want you to think that. I wasn't trying to do anything. It wasn't—" She stopped herself, closed her eyes, took a breath, and she reopened them, looking right at me. "I did not try to kill myself, nor did I want to. *But* I was sad, and when I found her, I laid down next to her." Her voice grew so hoarse. "I already knew she was gone and I wanted one more moment with her. When Ryan found me last summer, I was in the same position. It freaked him out."

"Mac," I could only whisper. "I only got through last year and leaving Cris because I knew you. Honest to God. You're one of the best friends I'll ever have. I knew that last year. I—I just meant to sort my shit out, get my head clear until I was good enough to come back. I knew if I hung out with you again, I'd see Ryan, and seeing Ryan. . . Yeah. I wasn't ready to deal with that, but in the back of my head, you were here. I relied on that to be true and the thought of you not being here, please don't ever do that. You can never leave."

Her eyes opened wide, filling with tears. She rushed over to me, wrapping her arms around me. "And I won't. I promise." She squeezed me so tight before sitting back so I could see her eyes again. "I got sad last summer, and I'll admit that if Ryan hadn't freaked out, if no one noticed, I could've gone back to that place. But he did notice, and he did freak out, and it jarred me. I don't ever want him to deal with my baggage." She glanced away.

I frowned. "Why not? I mean, you deal with his."

She looked back, frowning too. "What do you mean?"

I laughed abruptly, then quieted because it looked like she really hadn't thought of it that way. "Rispins. What she did. It was because of Cahill, because of the team. Because of Ryan's life, how it's going to be for him. How it already is. Fame. Popularity. Press. Girls. I know there was stuff that happened in high school. He's not even in the NBA yet. It's going to get bigger. He's going to get bigger and you're going to be at his side, dealing with your share of it. There's collateral damage both ways, on both parties. You deal with his stuff too."

Her eyebrows pulled together. "You're right. I never thought of it that way."

I reached for her hand, squeezing it, and wrapped my arm around her shoulders. I just wanted my friend next to me. "I want to help, in whatever way you need me to help. If you're willing to talk about it, I'd like to understand."

She stiffened before lifting her head up.

I couldn't identify the look on her face, as she blinked a few times.

I frowned. "What?"

"Ryan's the only one who's asked to understand it."

Oh. Oh no. "Is that—wrong?" I began to pull my hand away.

"No." She grabbed my hand. "It would mean the world to me, for you to want to understand."

"Well, yeah. I mean, if someone gets an injury and you're a part of their wellness team, you need to understand the injury to know how to help. I just think of it in those terms."

A tear rose up, resting on the bottom of her one eyelid, and she gave me another one of those smiles, the ones that yanked on my heartstrings. "I'd love to tell you." Her tear fell, right as she laughed lightly. "But we should schedule that because that could get heavy. Schedule that with maybe wine and we could dress in yeti costumes."

"Yeti costumes?"

"Yeah. So we can scare people on campus right after because that shit would be fun."

I laughed, thinking about it. "We should start with Kellie Rispins first."

She barked out a laugh. "Can you imagine us driving in the car there?"

"We'd get pulled over."

"The dogs in the cars next to us at stoplights. They'll go crazy."

"Right. The person driving needs to take the head off."

I started giggling at that statement itself.

Mac began laughing along with me, and we started to talk about if both of us should do yeti costumes or if one should do a unicorn costume.

I voted for yeti.

Mac voted to be the unicorn.

It felt appropriate.

"I'm sorry I went away," I murmured when the laughter faded.

She murmured right back, "I'm sorry I let you go away."

I rested my head against hers. "That's never going to happen again."

I meant it.

# 16

# MAREN

Things were heavy when Ryan and Cris got out of their practice.

I knew Ryan was heading to our dorm room to check on Mac, but Cris sent me a text.

**Cris: Where are you?**

**Me: At my room with Mac. I think Ryan's heading over.**

**Cris: He is. I'm not far behind him. I want to see you.**

**Me: Okay.**

There were conversations to have. Things to talk about. He needed to know about the article and about what all was going to be in there, and why it was coming out, but in all honesty, I knew Mackenzie would fill Ryan in and Ryan would fill Cris in. It's how their dynamic worked.

I wasn't sure what I was reeling about the most. About what happened to Cris, about Mackenzie, or how I could've been with Cris the entire time if I hadn't buckled under Kellie Rispins' threats.

It wasn't long until Ryan showed up, told me that Cris was waiting in the parking lot, and when I got out there, he was leaning against the outside of his truck. More than a few girls were watching him. A couple basketball groupies were heading his way, eyes on their target, so I intercepted them, getting in front and Cris pushed off from the truck, his eyes darkening on me.

"Hey," he said as I got closer, stopping with a few inches between us. We almost looked ridiculous, but I didn't care. If I leaned forward, my front would be touching his and so forth. Right now, we were both waiting. Holding back. His hands were inside his pockets.

I tipped my head back, my body buzzing from being so close to him. "Hey."

His eyes flashed. One of his hands lifted, touching my chin before he sighed and shook his head, stepping back. "Come on." He gestured to the truck. "I want to feed you."

My stomach growled, and I realized I hadn't eaten at all today.

Then again, I started the day hung over so I hadn't wanted to eat.

Cris watched as I got in and clicked my seat belt, and then we were off.

"Where are we going?"

"You'll see. Ryan and I grab food there quite a bit. They've got some of the best food around."

Even there, that felt right, finding out where he liked to eat.

It was information that I didn't know from last year.

A new wave of sadness rolled through me.

"You want to talk?"

I shook my head, resting my head back against the seat and looking at him. "Would you think less of me if I said no? There's a lot of heavy shit that went down today. Unless you want to? If you want to talk about how you're feeling, I'm here. Whenever."

We were at a stoplight so he gazed at me longer than normal. Studying me. "No. We don't have to talk."

I let out a sigh. "There's things I need to tell you, things you need to be prepared for—"

"Maren," he said softly.

"What?"

"I already know."

I frowned. "About the article?"

He nodded. "Mac called Ryan when you were heading to see Rispins. They had a full conversation about it, about what else she was going to have Troy put in the article."

"So you already knew?" My tongue felt so heavy. "About Mackenzie?"

"Yeah." We started forward again, the light changing, but he glanced back again. "I got the rundown when Coach called us in. He wanted to know everything that was going on."

I was trying to remember when Mac would've had time to call Ryan, but she had stepped outside when we were finishing up at Troy's house.

"What'd your coach say?"

"He was pissed, and he's going to make some calls, see if there's something legally the team can do to keep Rispins away, though it sounds like she might not be a problem anymore."

I frowned before whispering, looking away, "I hope so."

Then the article would be worth it.

What I went through would be worth it.

What Mackenzie divulged would be worth it.

"Hey," I murmured as we parked on a side street.

"Yeah?"

"Could we not—would it be okay if we didn't have *any* heavy talks tonight?"

Cris looked at me, long and intensely again, before a tenderness came over him. "Yeah. How about you just let me take care of you tonight?"

My throat swelled up, because God, he used to say that to me when we were hooking up. It was a joke between us, who'd take care of the other, and the joke was that it was a moot point. Cris took care of me. I took care of him. And then we'd take care of each other together all over again. But with him using those words, remembering, I felt some tears wanting to come to my eyes. I blinked them away, smiled, and said, "I'd really love that."

His eyes turned molten, and his voice dropped. "Good. Now, come on." He motioned with his head to a food truck.

As we got out, he took my hand, pulled me to his side, and dropped an arm around my shoulder. "See this place? It's the best chicken tacos in the area. You're going to never want chicken tacos anywhere else again."

My mouth was salivating, but it wasn't for the food. I was starving to have more of these experiences with Cris, to see him interact with the guys who owned the food truck, seeing how they knew him, seeing how they loved him. I wanted more of it. I wanted to catch up on all the memories I should've already known.

I wanted to fast track as if I wasn't relearning things about Cris, about Mac, and we were all on the same footing once more.

After we got our food, after we returned to the truck to eat, Cris was back to studying me again. Those long, intense perusals before he said, "Not going to break the no heavy talk rule, but I have to say—" He waited until my eyes turned so they were on his. A slow, wolfish grin spread over his face, a brief glimpse of some dark hunger flaring before he leaned over, finishing, "—that I'm goddamn fucking happy we went to find you last night at that bar."

Oh man.

A lump swelled up in the back of my throat, and I was forced to whisper around it, "Me too."

His mouth took mine, and it wasn't long before we were

both groaning, and before Cris was pulling back, growling. "Need to fuck you, right about *fucking* now."

I agreed, pressing against his side, as he clamped a hand on my leg and we tore out of there, heading for his house.

When we got there, his headlights lit on a person, Jude, who was leaning against the back of another truck in their driveway.

I jerked forward, frowning, but Cris braked suddenly and was out of the truck in a flash, biting out, "I don't think so."

He moved so fast.

I only had enough time to yell Cris' name before he was on Jude, and he slammed him up against the truck. "What *the fuck* are you doing here?"

"Hey. Whoa." The door to the front of the house opened and a bunch of guys rushed past me, running up and grabbing Cris. Two pulled him back while another stood in front of Jude. "What's going on?"

A truck pulled up behind us, parking, and Ryan got out, joining the group. He scanned the group before focusing on Cris. "Dude."

"I don't know. We just pulled in and the assface was here."

"Yeah!" Jude strained against the one guy holding him back, against his one hand. "I'm here because my girlfriend got me kicked out of my band. Mine."

Cris went still, his eyes narrowing.

The way he was watching Jude, like he wanted to tear his head off.

"She's not your girlfriend." Cris started for him again, but his two roommates quickly converged together, blocking him.

Ryan moved to the middle, his head back, studying Cris, and Jude started yelling again. Rotating, moving so fast, just like Cris had, Ryan had Jude against the truck again.

One of the guys moaned. "Not my truck. Please. My baby there."

Maybe hearing him, probably not, Ryan switched Jude, literally taking his shirt in two hands and throwing him down on the driveway. "You need to go. *Now*."

He stalked after him, an entire storm on his face, and Jude saw it, his protest swallowed as he thought better of whatever he was going to say. He scrambled backwards, but he didn't have enough time to get up. Ryan was there, on him again, and looking like he could commit any acts of violence on the guy. "I don't give a fuck why you're here. You will never come back here. You will never talk to anyone that's here, including my girl. Including Maren. Are you hearing me?"

Another growl burst from the side, and I started to look back, but Cris was past me. He was going for Jude too, except Ryan caught him, standing in his way.

"I want you gone. Wrong day to pick a fight." That was from Cris, snapping, and raking both of his hands through his hair. He pushed forward again, but Ryan turned all the way, shoving him back. "Stop."

Cris thrust a hand in the air, in Jude's direction. "I want him gone. Right the fuck now."

Jude finally got to his feet, and he started toward them. Then stopped as both Cris and Ryan turned to him, warning scowls on their faces.

My heart was tight right now. Clenched.

That dynamic between the two of them. I loved hanging out with them last year. Loved it so much. I never had a group of friends in high school where I felt accepted. I'd been there on the party scene, but on the fringes. There were core groups, core friends. I'd never been included, until last year with Mackenzie, Ryan, and Cristiano.

I missed so many months, and I missed them with him. I refocused on Jude, seeing he was struggling. He liked to be the epitome of cool, but he wasn't. Not among these guys. This group was on a different level, or at least Ryan and Cris were.

The stakes were higher for them where they either buckled under them or they met the pressure and rose above. So far, they had risen above. Jude was seeing this, eyeing both Cris and Ryan with a look of surprise.

I shook my head, moving toward them. "What did you want to accomplish coming here?"

Cris tensed, while Ryan looked back at me slowly.

Jude's eyes jerked to mine, and the same anger he had before rose over him. He stood as tall as he could, lifting his chin, his eyes burning. "I—you—they were my band! Mine, Maren. They kicked me out, and I know it was because of you."

He started to take a step toward me, but at Cris' one warning growl, he bounced in place, staying where he was. I came to stand on Cris' other side, and he shifted, his arm pressing against mine. It wasn't tension that left me, feeling his touch. Some of my same sadness was still there, but at his graze, some of it lifted. He was there to support me.

In one day, so much had changed.

I glanced up, sharing a look with him, before Jude yelled, "I want you to talk to them. Luis. Troy. Bannon. Make them take me back. They kicked me out because I was fucking Toya and that wasn't fair. You and I were never exclusive."

"You just called her your girlfriend." Their other room-mates had migrated down the driveway, one said that.

I shook my head. "We were never exclusive. We—just—" I glanced back at Cris for a second. "It was just a hook-up arrangement." I said to Jude, "Troy's not in the band."

"Does it matter? He may as well be."

True. He had a point. Luis did whatever Troy said. It's how they worked. I nodded slightly. "Fair enough, but they were looking for a reason to kick you out."

"Hell Skate is my band. I started it."

"So take the name and start a new band. They already mentioned it. Go away, Jude."

Hurt shone in his eyes, just briefly.

I felt bad. Or, I almost felt bad. Jude was dirty. Him still hooking up with Toya while he was hooking up with me and not telling me, douche move, but I never loved Jude. It's why I picked him. He was from a whole different world, one that I enjoyed because of the music. I could get lost in it just as much as him. But I was using him and he always knew it.

Other than his dirty factor, his worst traits were being a diva for the band. He'd been easy-going with me, chill to hang out with, and he kept his drama to what he really loved: the music. Thinking all of that, seeing him watching me, I pressed against Cris' side and gave Jude a small smile. "Pick your battles, Jude." Cris' arm slid around my waist, his hand anchoring on my hip and moving low. Jude saw it, his eyes following Cris' hand. I added, tilting my head to the side, "You weren't working with the guys and you know it. Take the name and move on. You did it once, you can do it again."

His mouth pursed, and he seemed to be considering it, his head cocking up as well. "You know what? You're right. I can do that. And I'll find better guys."

Doubtful. Luis was the best drummer around, but I just nodded. "You sure will."

"I will." He dipped his head before taking a step backwards. "I'm sorry for—I don't know why your boyfriend rushed me, but while I'm glad I came here, I'm sorry for the hostility." His eyes held to mine, lingering, and some resignation filtered in. "I hope you stop running from whatever you were trying to hide from, Maren. I did care about you."

"I know," I said softly. "If we hadn't cared a little, we wouldn't have used each other how we did."

He coughed slightly. "Yeah." He dipped his head down to Cris and Ryan before leaving, walking down one of the sidewalks.

"Did that dude walk here?" from one of their roommates.

I sank into Cris' side even more, laughing a little. "I wouldn't be surprised."

"Huh. Okay then. Fireworks over?" They went inside, leaving Ryan, Cris, and me.

Ryan and Cris shared another look before Ryan's gaze found mine, and seeing there was still a fire burning in his gaze, I readied myself, not sure if I wanted to hear whatever he was about to drop, because that was the look he had on his face.

I straightened up.

"I wasn't here for the start, but I can guess what happened before I showed up. If you don't ask, he won't tell you." He was referencing Cris. "But if Mac dumped me, then began hooking up with a guy, and I had to see that shit, and then when I got my girl back, and that same dude came around—I can tell you that the guy wouldn't be walking away looking like he's about to fucking start whistling. Just saying."

I felt slapped by those words.

He went inside, and I tipped my head back so I could see Cris better. "Where?"

Where had he seen Jude and me?

"I thought we—we were in another world. Jude and his band, that was another world. It's why—"

"Yeah." He glanced down, his jaw clenching. "The music world."

Exactly, but...

Oh.

Oh, no.

I remembered.

Cris loved music as well. It's another one of the reasons we got along, debating the classics. He mentioned taking an independent study in music. "You signed up for that class?"

"I signed up for that independent study. Needed a professor who'd work with my basketball schedule."

God. "So you saw us there?"

His jaw clenched again. "Saw enough." He glanced in the direction Jude had gone, and I felt the simmering heat come from him. "Saw enough to know that I'll never listen to that douche's music."

Guilt pressed down on all the other emotions already there, taking root in me, and none of them were going to move away until I processed it all. This, right now, this would've been a time when I needed to numb myself. With sex. With alcohol. With other things. Whatever worked.

Feeling all of it in me, hurting me, I rasped out, "If I could go back—"

"No." Cris moved in, his front against my front, and he leaned his forehead to mine. His body was so tight, so tense. His own tension making him feel like cement. "Listen." A woosh of air left him, and with that so much of his tension left. His hand lifted, cupping the side of my face. He said softly, "I don't do regrets. Okay? Don't let that shit fester in you. I had an uncle who lived only in regret. I don't think it helped him, so I hate that emotion. I won't feel it, and I don't want you to feel it. What happened, happened. The only good thing about looking back is learning how to do things better. Let's do that instead?" His head lifted, his eyes still holding mine.

No regret? I drew in a shuddered breath. "I don't know if I can do that."

"Then I'll help you. Let me help you."

I nodded, taking that from him, knowing I *could* take that from him.

He cradled my face in both of his hands, his thumbs smoothing down over my cheeks. "You good?"

No. But I said, "Getting there."

"Good." He dipped his head down again, his mouth finding mine, and just like in his truck, the desire didn't take long to build. A deep groan left him as he bent, his hands falling from my face, going to my ass, and he lifted me up.

My arms and legs went around him, and he carried me to his bedroom.

I'd had sex with Cris a lot, but this night was different.

It was more.

It was deeper.

I was pretty sure it was with love.

# 17

# MAREN
## STILL LATER.

The response to the article was overwhelming. It was mostly good, turning so many things upside down. There was some bad, but it was how the world worked. There'd always be bad. I only focused on the good, and a big good thing that happened was that Kellie was kicked out of school.

I rolled over in bed with Cris one night. "Tell me again what Cahill said to Ryan."

That was another of the changes that happened.

He shrugged, lying beside me with one of his arms around me. His other hand was playing with mine, and he was looking up at his ceiling. "You get off on this shit, don't you?" He glanced down at me.

I gave him a wolfish grin. "Maybe."

He snorted, grinning. "Cahill was pissed when he found out about that article, and I mean pissed. His parents are suing her because he never wanted Ryan off the team. He was just an asshole, wanting to be top dog. That's it. Ryan is the reason he didn't go pro early, because he knew with him joining, we could win March Madness. The team came so close last year."

"Is that really true? Cahill really didn't want Ryan off the team?"

"Yeah. He never did. He just wanted to make sure Ryan wasn't top dog. But fuck, that article has people looking at him so sideways."

"I do wonder why she did it for him, though. If she wanted him? Or if there was another reason?"

"She didn't say?"

I shook my head. "It seems the interview he did to clear up his side was pointless."

"Goes to show you how damning words can be, because no one believes that Cahill was another victim in all of this too."

"The lawsuit might help."

He grunted. "No one's going to care. People have made up their minds, and not only does everyone love Ryan, everyone loves his girlfriend."

I smiled, snuggling even closer to him, one of my legs tangling with his. "That's the best part."

"Yeah," he said softly. "That is."

Everyone rallied around Mackenzie. Almost literally.

She broke everyone's hearts, anyone who read the article, then clicked to learn about her sister's story. The university reached out to her because they wanted to discuss if she'd be interested in becoming the face of their advocacy and student hotline program.

Local and national news asked to do interviews with her. Major outlets, like *Good Morning America*. Ryan Jensen drew everyone in, and then they looked next to him to where Mackenzie stood, and they fell in love.

"I don't understand that feeling. I don't know why. I just can't, but I'd have to imagine that it's one of the worst feelings to experience, of not wanting to be here anymore."

We had our talk. Mac and me. I asked her questions, and she answered them. I worried if I would trigger her again. If I'd be too much with all my questions, but she shook her head and said, "*No*. We're told to talk about our issues, if we're struggling with something except about this. It means the world that you're asking because you want to learn. I will sit here for days answering your questions because that's how grateful I am."

I didn't understand why she was saying that, but I thought about it a lot.

I said to Cris now, "Everyone wants to be understood. Right?"

I felt him start to frown, but he didn't comment. He knew this was something where I wasn't really talking to him. I was more talking to figure something out.

"I kinda wonder if it's like a train where it's only going off of a cliff. She's on it, but she can't get off on any of the stops. If she does, either people have their backs to her or she's going to be met by other scary people. So because of that, she can't get off on any of the stops until it's the end where she knows it's going off a cliff so she has to jump at the end—"

"Okay." Cris rolled over on top of me. "Enough with the train analogy."

"I'm trying to understand."

He propped himself up, his eyes gentling. "I know, and that makes you a good friend to her."

"It's because she's a good friend to me."

"I know that too, but I think another way you can think of it is that if she's struggling, the pressure will build and build and it would help if she had someone to talk to, because when she does that, some of the pressure releases. Maybe that's a better way of thinking of it?"

That made so much sense. "Like she's a balloon and she keeps getting air pumped inside of her, and the balloon keeps stretching and stretching until it's going to po—"

"Stop." His eyes flashed, but the corner of his mouth tugged up in a grin. "No matter what, being able to talk about whatever is going on with you is always good."

I rolled my head back on the pillow. "How'd you get so wise about topics like this?" A horrible thought came to me, and horror began filling me up. "You're not—"

"No."

The horror stopped, and it deflated. Like a balloon.

"But," he said quietly. "I'm a guy and I'm lucky to have a good family, good brothers, and a great best friend. I can talk to them about shit, about how I feel. A lot of guys don't and it's not because they choose not to, because it's not manly or something. Though, that way of thinking doesn't help either. It's because men don't know how to talk about their feelings. They don't know what they're feeling. Growing up, we're taught we can feel three things: lust, anger, and hunger. That's it. There's a lot of lonely guys out there."

I had to ask because it was now making me feel a certain way. "You? Are you one of them?"

He gazed down at me, his eyes darkening. "No," he said softly again. He shifted so one of his hands rested on the side of my face, and he brushed some of my hair back. He did it so tenderly. Loving. "Remember that uncle I mentioned before? The one who could only live in regret?"

I nodded, seeing a different, more somber look come over him. "Yeah."

"He killed himself and it made me rethink a lot of shit in life. It made my brothers and I decide to grow up differently."

"Oh."

"I'm okay. I am. I—I don't want to get into all of that, but I was just saying that it made me look at life differently. My brothers and I are close. I don't know if we would've been otherwise." His gaze slipped to the side.

I reached up, touching the side of his face. "Hey."

He looked back, his eyes warming.

I said, lightly. "I'm glad you have a good relationship with your brothers."

"Me too." He grinned, but it didn't quite meet his eyes. "After that article came out, you and I haven't really talked about us."

My chest swelled up.

He wanted to have that conversation now?

Was it too late to call Mac up for another drive around town in our yeti and unicorn costumes?

"You look so panicked." He'd been watching my face.

I made it go blank before—fuck it. I let him see my fear. That was the whole theme here, being authentic and shit. No more running. No more hiding. No more going numb. "I know we started this whole thing, you and me, and it was supposed to be fun. Light and fun, and no strings. But I saw you those three times and—" I tried looking away.

He tipped my head right back, his palm cupping the side of my face.

It felt so warm. He felt so warm.

I drew that in and let it steady me. "I can't do the no strings again." Oh, boy. The tears were coming back. I tried blinking them away. "It has to be exclusive or..." My heart was pounding so hard, so loud. "Or I can't do this with you. I feel like I should apologize for this change, but I'm not going to apologize. It's how I feel and I have to be true to how I feel. I'm standing my ground, in my truth, or whatever that saying is. In the sand of truth or—fuck if I know. You know what I mean."

"You're standing your ground?" His voice came out in a low growl.

Oh, God. That wasn't good.

I gulped. "Yep. Still standing in the sand of trust, or tree of truth, or—shit!"

"You're firm on that. That's what you're saying?"

My eyes met his. "Yeah. As firm as your dick when you're railing me."

His entire face twitched before he cursed under his breath. "Jesus Christ, Maren. You drive me fucking crazy."

My heart was going to be ripped to pieces. I felt the first tear coming.

He suddenly rolled us in his bed, with me on top, with my legs straddling him, and he shoved down his pants, bringing me on top of him. And because we'd had sex not long ago, I hadn't pulled on my panties, so when he pulled me down, he thrust up into me.

I cried out from how quick it happened, and then I moaned because holy damn, that felt really good. "What does this mean?"

A savage growl burst from him as he held my hips down and started thrusting up into me.

Christ. I was bouncing. My tits were going everywhere, but he caught one in his teeth, biting down on me. I screamed, arching my back. Hot pleasure surged through me, coating me.

I had no idea what was happening. My mind was scrambled, but we were having sex and Cris was really worked up, going at me in a frenzy.

"Cris," I groaned.

"What?" he growled.

"What does this mean?"

"You want me to stop?"

I clamped down tighter on him, my legs squeezing him at the same time.

"Oh, fuck." He went still until I let him go, and he began grinding against me. Into me.

"Cris," I gasped, already feeling the beginning of my release.

Jesus, no. It was too soon. Too quick. If this was the end of us, I wanted to last as long as possible.

"You're asking what this means?" he clipped out, sitting up, wrapping an arm around my back and holding me in place, but now his chest was to my chest. His mouth dipped, finding mine. His tongue swept in. "All of that bullshit from last year. You leaving me because some bitch made you scared. Not telling me. Not letting me have a say. You doing it thinking to save me. Then that same bitch fucks with my head, and fucks me, and I find out that I lost you, thinking I just had you, and then I'm seeing you fucking around with some punk loser?"

"Where are you going with this?" I was still moaning.

I needed to slow my climax. Stop it.

*Grandma, grandma, grandma.*

Nope. It wasn't working. He was still pumping furiously up into me, his tongue claiming me at the same time. He nipped at the corner of my mouth. "Look at me."

I looked at him, more because I was shocked at the gruff command.

His eyes were heated and blazing. He caught the side of my face, holding me in place as he slammed up into me. "You're saying 'your truth' now like I've not been here. Like I didn't walk into that bar, sling you over my shoulder and carry you out, or like I didn't make you sleep in my bed when you were throwing attitude at me left and right the night before, and getting sick eight hundred fucking times."

My eyes went wide. Eight hundred? No wonder it was the hangover of all hangovers.

He kept going, still growling, but he nipped at the other corner of my mouth, still holding my face in place. "I was with you all the next day. At your side. Following you, thinking I was going to end up delivering you back to your boyfriend's door, no matter that you gave me that 'come hither and fuck me good' look that you did when you sauntered into the shower. Or that I had to have seconds because I didn't know when or if I'd get to taste you again. Or all of the shit that happened afterwards when I realized I stuck my dick in someone I would never want to stick my dick into. But after your whole train analogy of needing to talk about our emotions, I know that I'm going to need to face whatever that event makes me feel. But I will because I'm not letting you not be at my side. Like I've been at your side every single day. Every single night, you're in my bed or I'm in yours. And you're now just giving me the exclusive or nothing talk like you think you're delivering a death sentence to you and me?"

I was so confused, but God, he was blasting my body with some serious carnal and primal delicious sensations. I wasn't complaining.

He rolled us again, with him on top, still in me, and he paused. He arched over me, lifting his head so he could see me. So I could see him, and my breath stopped, holding in my chest at the look in his eyes. They were shining, they were so bright.

The hand that cupped the side of my face gentled, matching his tone. "I don't know how else to show you I love you without actually just saying the words."

I went still.

His thumb went to my bottom lip, running over it. He kept watching me, reading into me. "We started with laughter and no strings, but that changed the night you were here when I found out my sister lost her baby. That night I started sinking into you, and I've never looked back. I messed up, though, because I never told you that. I'm sorry. So here it is, my truth. I love you. I started falling in love with you almost a full year ago today. Homecoming weekend. That's when I would've had a new niece. Instead, I got you and I forgot that you don't read minds. So fuck no to you walking from me. I love you, and that for damn sure means no other chick or dick is going to touch you because you're mine. You hear me?" He leaned down, drilling his words into me.

I responded by opening my legs wider for him, and he groaned, his eyes rolling backwards. "Fuck me."

I pushed up, my hips raising to start hitting against his, and I growled as I nipped the side of his mouth. "That's the idea, because you're mine right back, Chavez."

A whole new rumble came out of him as I used his last name. He picked up his pace, and so did I, rolling with him until we both collapsed, releasing together.

It was fucking perfect.

No. Wait.

I looked over at him, panting, trying to catch my breath. "I love you too."

He went still, looking over, and a new tenderness came over him as he lifted himself up, moving to kiss me. "Thank God because if you didn't, I was just going to keep fucking you until you did."

I grinned against his lips.

Okay.

Now it was perfect.

# EPILOGUE
## MACKENZIE

*Christmas Season.*

"What's your favorite Christmas song?" I asked as Ryan was bringing out the last of the decorations for the party he and his roommates were having at their house. I was in charge of the playlist, which was probably for the best, because when I tried baking, everything got burned. When I tried decorating, things got broken.

Ryan eventually picked me up so I didn't cut my feet on the glass, sat me on the couch, and gave me this latest assignment.

So far I was finding out that there weren't a lot of Christmas songs that I enjoyed. I was pretty sure that said something about myself, but I didn't want anyone to know.

"Um." Ryan was distracted, untangling a string of lights that had been already untangled, until I touched them. That was it. That was all I did. I picked them up, and voila, they were all tangled up once more. We were going on day two of decorating the house. Their roommates did the basement yesterday, and

Chavez and Ryan were doing the main floor today. The party was tomorrow. "I don't know. 'Little Drummer Boy'?'

"What?" I jerked upright on the couch.

"What?" He gave me a look in return.

"Why that song?"

He frowned. "Is there something wrong with that song?"

"No." I pulled it up and clicked on it. The beginning filled the room and I contemplated what drew Ryan to this song. "Is it because it's about a boy?"

He snorted a laugh. "I don't know. It's the first one that popped in my head. I've never really thought about Christmas songs. That time of the year is usually a fucking mess. Finals. Parties. Then we got training and games when everyone else leaves. I'm not a big holiday person, Mac. You know that."

I did. I lay back down, going through more songs. "Everyone seems to like 'Silent Night'?"

He smothered a laugh, getting the lights untangled again so he laid them down. "Why are you saying it like that? Are you questioning why so many people like it?"

"I don't know." And I didn't. "Willow was the one who liked the holidays so much."

He paused, and I felt his eyes on me. "So what was Willow's favorite Christmas song?"

Pain seared me. It was brief, but intense. I swallowed over a knot. "I don't know." I didn't like that I didn't know, but I was remembering. "It changed every year. She usually got obsessed with whatever music artist that was popular that year and if they put out a Christmas album."

Why was this bugging me?

Willow was fickle, but not about the holidays. It was the only time of the year when she wasn't so hard on herself. When she smiled, and it felt genuine. I murmured, almost to myself, "She liked Halloween because it was an excuse to dress sexy and no one could say anything about it. She loved going to school Halloween week in a new sexy outfit every day, and she really loved that the principal couldn't tell her to go home and change outfits."

"You guys did costumes every day of the week?"

"No, just Willow's friends. They were the popular group. They got away with anything they wanted to do."

"What about Christmas? What's your favorite Christmas song?" He came over, staring down at me as he asked.

My tongue swelled up. "I don't know."

"You don't know?"

There was that feeling again. Why didn't I want to admit that I didn't really like any of the songs? What did that say about me?

"Everyone has at least one song they don't mind hearing. What's the first one that comes to your mind?"

I couldn't answer because my mind went blank. That was Willow's holiday. Easter was hers too. Fourth of July. All the popular holidays were hers.

"What's going on in your head? He came over and lifted me up, sat down and brought me to his lap. I stretched out, getting comfortable.

"They're Willow's."

"What's Willow's?"

"The holidays. The songs. She made us listen to whatever was her favorite song over and over again." I'd forgotten about all of this. "None of us ever complained. That's not normal. We should've complained or fought with her about the songs, because honestly, some of them were so annoying."

His arms tightened around me. The scent of his shampoo drifted over me, covering me, and I relaxed even more. Evergreen pine. God, I loved that smell. It reminded me of when we used to walk among the trees, looking for the one we'd put up in the house, but that was back when we used real trees. We switched to fake trees so long ago, but I missed that smell.

"So why didn't you guys complain?"

The answer was so simple to me, and I wished that I had realized it back then. "She was happy." Images flashed in my mind, when she declared she got radio privileges in the car. As she put the holiday music on in the kitchen and danced through, laughing, her hair flowing behind her. When we'd go to open gifts and Willow showed up, suddenly so determined that we needed to set the mood. We needed the perfect song, those were always her words.

Music meant so much to her, and I hadn't known. I hadn't realized at the time.

"She was happy," I repeated, a soft sigh leaving my body, some unknown tension unwinding from me. I wasn't sad thinking about it. It made sense now. I waited, expecting some regret to flare through me, but it didn't come. Just acceptance. "She was different during holidays, when it was just the family. She was different around her friends and her boyfriend, more guarded. Tense. But she was always like that. Except with Christmas music. She needed the right song for every event. Decorating the tree. When we opened gifts. When we ate breakfast Christmas morning. She loved setting the mood. That's what she said, but she was happy when she did. She was just her. She was only a teenager when she did that so we let her. No one complained."

The holidays were hers. The Christmas songs were hers.

I added, "I never minded. What made her happy made me happy." Why was I only now thinking about all of this? But then again, did it matter? "I don't have a favorite song, Ryan."

"Do you want a favorite song?"

I considered it and nodded, feeling like I was confessing as I said, "Yeah. I think I do. Maren said a Christmas song is a song that's supposed to make you happy. I'm guessing she meant a favorite song."

"Okay. Let me look at the ones you compiled." He took my

phone and began going through my playlist, then laughed. "Mac."

"What?"

"These are horrible song choices."

I groaned, pressing my nose into his shoulder. "Why am I so bad at this stuff?"

He was starting to curate my list, adding other songs to it, and he rubbed a hand down my back at the same time. "You just said it yourself. Holidays were your sister's thing."

I was looking at the new songs he was picking.

Silver Bells.

White Christmas.

Carol of the Bells.

I Want a Hippopotamus for Christmas.

Please Come Home for Christmas by the Eagles.

Believe by Josh Groban.

You're a Mean One, Mr. Grinch.

You Make It Feel Like Christmas.

O Holy Night.

Mary, Did You Know?

Do You Hear What I Hear?

I sighed. "You're so good at that." As I kept watching, he made different playlists. One was for the party. Another was more emotional songs. And there were others, the classics.

Rudolph the Red-Nosed Reindeer was on that one. Frosty the Snowman. Blue Christmas by Elvis. Last Christmas. Christmas Canon. It's Beginning to Look A Lot Like Christmas. Santa Baby.

He was picking and choosing so fast.

"Wait. Click on that one." I pointed at one.

He frowned, glancing at me. "'The Season's Upon Us' by Dropkick Murphys?"

I nodded and got comfortable as the song came over the

room. Ryan synced it to the speakers throughout the entire house, and as it sounded around us, he kept scrolling.

"Oh! Click on that one."

He gave me another look. "'An Irish Pub Song' by The Rumjacks?"

"Yeah. That one."

"That's not a Christmas song."

I frowned, thought about it, and shrugged. "Click on it anyways."

He snorted, but did and soon that song was sounding through the house. I had a sudden inclination to buy a bunch of mugs and plaster the word 'filthy' over them, then hand them out for the party tomorrow.

Feliz Navidad came on next.

"What's that one?"

He clicked on it, and soon I was hearing about an Italian Christmas donkey. I said, "Add that to one of the party playlists."

He laughed again, but did it.

I liked this. I lay on Ryan's lap as he went through more songs. They had put their tree up this morning and strung lights all around the main floor, so as we sat there, it got dark outside and the lights clicked on since everything was set to an automatic schedule. I grew tired, lazy, and started to drift off when Cris came in. "Yo!" He walked into the living room, saw me, and lowered his voice. "Oh, shit. Sorry."

"She's fine. Just dozing. Everything set outside?"

"Yeah, yeah. We only need to set up the inflatables and go over the drinks."

"We can get all the drink stuff in the morning after practice. Are we good with inflatables? Do we need to get more, or do we have enough?"

"We've got three Santas. A Bumble inflatable. Reindeer. A

shit ton of Christmas tree inflatables. A minion one. And, uh. . . What else?"

"Christmas flamingos."

"Yes. Those too. Oh, and all those extra candy cane inflatables. Easterly, Grant, and Cahill are coming over in the morning to do the snacks too."

Ryan laughed under his breath. "Jesus. Can't believe that's happening."

"What?" Chavez half-laughed too. "That your previous sworn enemy is helping throw a holiday party with us?"

"Exactly."

"Well, it's a whole team event and Coach is giving us a day off, so fuck yeah, let's party. After everything that went down this year, we deserve to celebrate a little. Plus, shit's going to be crazy when we go into January and for March Madness. You know all eyes are going to be on our team."

Ryan tensed underneath me, and I shifted, but suddenly he was lifting me up and he moved so he was sprawled across the couch. He laid me on top of him, on my stomach, and I burrowed again into his chest and shoulder.

"What are you doing?" Cris asked.

"Making a bunch of playlists. Mac was going to make us listen to 'Mary, Did You Know?' during the party tomorrow."

He snorted out a half-smothered laugh. "What?"

Ryan sighed, but said fondly, "If she ever starts thinking about becoming a party planner, we all need to gently dissuade that idea."

Chavez laughed again. "Finally. One area your girl doesn't dominate in."

I was so awake for this conversation, and I was mentally preening. *Please, say more about me. Let's hear all the good stuff.*

I heard the click on my phone as Ryan must've changed the songs again. A different one came through the speakers.

"Who's that one by?" Cris asked.

"Tom Walker. 'For Those Who Can't Be Here.'" Ryan ran a hand down my side before getting up. "Let's do those inflatables downstairs. We won't have to worry about them tomorrow, and I don't know what you and Maren are doing tonight, but I want to reserve the basement. Mac wants to do Christmas movies tonight."

"That sounds fun. Is that a you-two thing, or could Maren and I join?" They went downstairs and their voices faded.

I rolled to my back, stretching out as I opened my eyes.

The room was magical with the soft glow of the lights, and just above on the ceiling, right where I lay, the guys had hung glowing snowflakes with rolls of cotton attached to the ceiling so it gave the idea it was snowing inside the room.

Ryan chose this song for me, letting me listen to it by myself.

*Willow...*

When I felt her in the past, I didn't know if it was her.

If she spoke in my head.

I had made the decision a long time ago that I didn't care. If I felt it was her, it was her. I wasn't going to second-guess it.

I picked up my phone, clicked on the song so it would repeat, and lay back down, listening to the words.

When I told my secret to my counselor, that the note wasn't Willow's, that it'd been mine, there was a freeing feeling I got. But I never told Maren last year.

In a way, I'd gone back into the closet. Ryan knew. My family knew. They were the only ones who mattered, or that's what I thought at the time.

This time was different.

I was approached by so many outlets for interviews, for advocacy options. I'd lost count of how many offers came in. It was all overwhelming, and I'd not made any decision because I wasn't sure what I wanted to do.

But people didn't hate me. They didn't blame me. They

didn't look at me like I was sick, or weak, or how Kellie thought about me. There were negative responses, but I didn't pay attention to them. The overwhelming majority was good.

It'd been me telling the world.

That'd been my truth, and it was out. I had nothing else holding me back, nothing else that I was hiding.

Listening to the song lyrics on repeat, I knew some of it wasn't accurate.

A buzzing sensation went through me, filling me up. It felt happy. It felt content. It felt like her.

Willow was listening to the song with me. She was here, I just couldn't see her.

I added the song to my personal folder that was titled, *Songs for Willow*. It might be her new favorite one. And just then, the decision to do the interviews clicked. I was going to do them. All of them. I was going to talk about my truth, and I was going to talk about Willow. It was going to be about both our journeys.

Willow mattered. I mattered.

It felt right.

It felt like it was my path to take.

# A VERY SMALL EPILOGUE
## RYAN

"What the fuck?" Cahill lifted up his mug the next night. "Jensen, why did your girlfriend give me this mug?"

I frowned.

She and Maren went shopping this morning, coming back with a ton of mugs they bought from a secondhand store. They'd taken over a table in the back room, with a label maker machine. I'd not paid attention, more so because Chavez and another of our roommates kept fighting over the amount of alcohol that should go into the punch bowl. I'd stood by in case they needed a referee because shit got serious between them.

"What does it say?" There was a label glued on the mug.

"It says Filthy Animal."

The fuck?

Easterly held his up. "Mine says Filthy Jerk."

Grant added, "Mine is Filthy Fella."

Chavez snickered, looking at his mug. "Filthy Horse's Ass. I have a filthy horse's ass mug."

Laughter burst from the corner, where Maren and Mackenzie stood, along with Lauren and a few other girls. Troy,

Luis, and their other two band members from that band, who the fuck knew what their names were because it seemed to have changed, all stood with them. All of them grinning or trying not to laugh, but then Mackenzie gave me a sly grin and pressed a button on her phone.

An Irish Pub Song by The Rumjacks played next.

I had a feeling Mac found her favorite holiday song.

For more stories, go to
www.tijansbooks.com

If you enjoyed this novella, please leave a review. They truly **help so much.**

# LINKS AND RESOURCES

https://www.crisistextline.org/
Text 741741 from anywhere in the USA to text with a trained
Crisis Counselor.

https://suicidepreventionlifeline.org
Call 1-800-273-8255 or if you go on their website, you can chat
online.

For more facts about suicide prevention
and warning signals, go to
http://www.211bigbend.org/nationalsuicidepreventionlifeline
or call 1-800-273-TALK

# ACKNOWLEDGMENTS

Thank you to all the readers who read and enjoyed Ryan and Mackenzie when Ryan's Bed first came out. I was so terrified to publish that story, and how the book has been treasured by so many has touched my heart in ways I could never explain.

I never intended to write a sequel, and this is not a sequel, but I never thought I could write something that would be what Ryan's Bed deserved for a sequel. That said, I did a poll in my reader group for what book they would like a special edition cover made for and they chose Ryan's Bed. So I decided to to also write bonus material to add to the special edition cover, but I was not expecting that when I started writing—I could't stop.

This novella was what came from that bonus material.

I know it was different with the two different couples, but I went with what was speaking to me. I hope the readers enjoyed this holiday novella.

Thank you to Crystal. Thank you to my editor and all my proofreaders. Thank you to Becca for fitting me in and rooting for Cris. And as always, thank you to the readers in my reader group and also to all those readers who keep enjoying my books.

And also, thank you to my pup Bailey.

# AVEKE

## CHAPTER ONE

He was here. Again.

This was, what? The fourth time this week. Eight sharp. The last four evenings in a row. And he came in, took the stool at the far end, and sat. Just sat. His head bowed. He took a breath before he lifted his head, and he paused, like he'd needed one second before readying to slip on the mask that the rest of the world saw. Then he tipped his head back, his eyes went to the television right above him, and as Brandon gave him a beer for the night, he'd sip and watch his best bud play soccer on the TV. And like tonight, if it weren't his best friend's team playing, we'd switch it to another game. Score if it was someone we knew playing, because around these parts, that wasn't that uncommon. But not tonight.

There was a hockey game, but not the team he liked to watch.

Brandon wasn't working tonight since I had told him twenty minutes ago that I'd close for him. Brandon had a woman, and he was happy, so he was starting to let me close most nights for him. So tonight, I moved down the bar, meeting Zeke's eyes briefly before he saw me reach for a tall glass and pour his favorite beer from the tap.

He was tired. I caught the wariness before he switched. A wall came over him, and then he reanimated to the cocky jerk that most people took Zeke Allen for being. Wealthy. Preppy. If that was still a descriptor for someone our age. We're in our twenties, so I suppose instead of preppy, we could use the word 'blessed' to describe him. He didn't seem like he aged.

Muscular. Big broad shoulders. He had the physique of a bodybuilder. Dark blond hair.

A very big square jawline, but it was so prominent, that it alone could get so many women in bed with him. I'd seen him in action many a night, and he never had to work hard. He tended to buy them a drink, ask them how they were, and within a few minutes (always depending on how long Allen wanted to chat), they'd head out.

Zeke was gorgeous when we were in high school, not that he and I attended the same school. With our neighboring towns, one could say I was on one side of the tracks and he was on the other. The privileged. He went to a private school, which seemed to get more private and exclusive as the years passed, and I was from Roussou. It used to be a good place, alive and thriving, and then it took a turn and not many seemed as privileged there anymore. I think it was doing better these last few years due to some local businesses that brought in a bunch of people, but still...it was hurting.

I finished his pour and took the remote for the television. Placing both before him, I gave him a nod. "Think Kansas City Mustangs are playing tonight."

He grunted, took a sip, and picked up the remote. "Thanks, Ava. Thinking I'd like to watch the Javalina tonight."

He was already changing the channel before I turned to fill another order.

I knew Zeke would sip his beer and want another in twenty

minutes. Then a third on the hour. He'd stay almost to closing, stopping long before he'd need to drive to sober up. Once a guy with the reputation for being a bully and an obnoxious jackass, he wasn't like that anymore.

Eyeing him from the corner of my eye, I wanted to ask what happened to change his ways. One day.

Check out the rest of Aveke
or go to www.tijansbooks.com

# HOCKEY WITH BENEFITS
## CHAPTER ONE

I liked hockey. I already knew it, but by the third period, I *really* knew it.

The wine might've been a factor, or the two beers that my roommate bought me, but either way, I was having fun. I had a new appreciation for the sport.

I was also enjoying watching Cruz Styles, the team's star player, zip around the rink like he'd been born on skates and not with two normal feet. He wasn't the only one, though. They were all going so fast, like they were flying on ice. It was exhilarating to watch. It wasn't my first hockey game, but it was my first hockey game at Grant West. Everyone on campus had been raving about the new guy for a while now.

His looks didn't hurt either.

His picture was flashed on the jumbotron so many times over the night that I'd lost count. It was having an effect on the three girls in front of me, and also in my vagina. With the hockey mask on, you could still see his fierce dark blue eyes. His high cheekbones. With the mask off, he had a whole chiseled jawline that wasn't legal. I swear. And those cheekbones were set high and wide, giving the sides of his face an indented look, but it worked on him. Not to mention the messy dark hair on top of his head and how he had the look where he could rifle his hand through it, let it go and he still looked fucking hot. Comb that shit back, put him in a suit, and he'd be giving off 007 vibes.

The guy wasn't just pretty. He was sizzling hot, and right now, he was whipping down the ice, going left, through two defenders, creating an opening to the goal and *bam*–the puck was slapped–*denied*. The goalie thrust his leg out, and the puck went off it, going behind the net.

It was picked up by the other team and sent sailing to the other side of the rink.

Off Cruz went, but he'd be back in two seconds because that'd been the theme of the night.

Grant West was pushing hard the whole night, but Cruz was leading the charge. Over and over again.

I was half winded just watching them.

"Yo." Miles Gaynor moved next to me, his shoulder lightly bumping into mine. "You know Race Ryerson?"

"What?" I was fully in a drunk haze, and I was enjoying it.

Miles had first been a class friend. Then a party friend. Now he was kind of a roommate. A little skinny, floppy brown hair, but where it looked cute on him, and baby fresh cheeks, the guy was a looker. It'd been because of him that I was living in my own little space in the attic of a house where he and his cousin, a guy from the football team, and a couple other girls all lived as well. They were all chill, but I'd only met them twice and hanging out at the hockey game was the second time of those two instances. When my roommate from first semester left college to pursue a job in her family business, I hadn't wanted to stick around and see who else my college chose to be her replacement. Hence, Miles.

He nodded to my left. "He's been staring over here at you almost the whole time. Isn't he with someone?"

I frowned, but looked around, the edges of my vision blurring before I focused and saw the guy Miles was talking about. At my look, he diverted his head, but bent down to his girlfriend, who was cheering for the team.

There went my nice buzz.

Tasmin Shaw and Race Ryerson.

As he talked to her, she stopped cheering, her smile falling as she leaned forward, her eyes searching, searching, and finding me. I frowned, narrowing my eyes, but she only went still before raising a hand up and giving me a slight wave and smile with it.

I scowled, but she barely blinked at that.

Goddamn.

"What's the deal there?"

I jerked forward, my whole body going stiff. "Nothing."

"He's never been a creep before."

"He's not. His girlfriend is next to him. Tasmin Shaw."

"So?"

I shrugged. "Taz is probably just confused why I moved out of the dorms. She lived across from me, that's all." I was lying because while she wasn't from my hometown, she knew people who were, and I was guessing that she'd heard the gossip. Her boyfriend too.

My phone buzzed, and I glanced at the screen.

**Kit: OMG! Your mom?! Are you okay?**

**Dad: Checking on you. Wanted to see how you're doing? I'm so sorry you're going through this. I know you like your space and you don't process like that, but I'm here if you want to talk. Any time, no matter what day or hour. Love you, honey.**

Nope. Kit was a friend from back home. Panic burst in my chest, right before everyone and everything began to swim around me. Turning my phone off, I refused to deal with what I knew that text was about, what the gossip that Taz and her boyfriend had heard about me. It'd been the catalyst of why I came to the game tonight. What my mom did earlier, why I panicked, drove three hours home and three hours back wasn't going to be dealt with tonight.

I wanted more to drink, and the sooner the better.

"OH!" His eyes got big, and his shoulders went low. "I didn't even think about that. Good to know. Just thought it was weird, that's all."

I fixed him with a look. "Look. You don't have to do this."

My stomach was swirling, and I wasn't getting a good feeling here. Miles and I partied. Sometimes we shared a table at the library, but that'd been the extent of our friendship. I had rules with friends, no personal questions. There was a reason for it, and it was significant. I was usually able to handle that rule with friends because so far, I picked the party crowd. Deep meaningful conversations weren't the norm. It was mostly drinking, flirting, all that jazz. Sometimes there was a catty comment from another girl, and I had a few run-ins. It happened with me, not because I sought them out but because a guy was hitting on me, and the girl got jealous. Guys liked my face. It was round, but my chin somewhat gave me a heart-shaped face. They also liked how my hazel eyes looked combined with my long cinnamon dark hair. Plus, the fact that I was tiny, petite, but I had a rack and some ass. I also had sex appeal, and the reason for that is because I enjoyed sex. God. With my life, it'd become my coping mechanism, but guys could sense that from me and that's what they were only interested in from me. Beyond that, I wasn't the girl that got the guy.

I knew the deal. The guys knew the deal. It was the other girls who didn't.

I was fine with the deal, not that I partook. That's just what the guys wanted from me, but it gave me space sometimes with people. But what Miles was bordering on was something that felt like what a friend would do for someone.

I didn't want those types of friends. Or, to be more accurate, I couldn't have those types of friends.

"What?"

"You. Me. This." I gestured to the roommates, and the game. "I've got walls. I know this. You know this. They're there for a reason. You don't owe me anything. You don't have to be protective because a guy is looking my way."

He took a step back, his tone coming out cold. "Fine. I just know we watch out for each other at parties. Didn't think it was different here, but cool. Good to know. I won't watch out anymore."

Crap.

He had me because he was right. We did do that.

"Miles," I started.

"I'm out of here." He pushed his hands in his pockets and shouldered through the crowd.

Another roommate came over. Wade Kressup, Miles' cousin. His gaze slid to where Miles had just disappeared before he bent down to me. I was almost a whole foot below him. "Do I ask?"

The buzzer went off, signaling the end of the game, and I shook my head. "Nope."

I sighed, needing to refocus my thoughts. I was off today.

I turned my phone back on long enough to send a text to Miles.

**Hey. Some stuff happened earlier today, and it was serious. I don't want to get into it, but it's no excuse. I'm sorry for being a bitch. Thank you for being you.**

Everyone was heading out, but I stayed for a beat. I needed to get grounded. Too many emotions I was trying to ignore and thoughts I was trying not to think were creeping in. Add to all that, I'd been a bitch to a friend and yeah. . . I wasn't doing so well on being a decent human being here.

The whole day had gotten away from me.

My chest felt like it was being sucked out of me.

It took me a little bit before I realized Cruz was down on the ice. He was staring up at me and he half raised one of his gloves up. I gave him a small nod right back. Which, okay, I was down for what he was asking to do. Because that whole gesture was an invitation, but also crap, because that meant I'd have to turn my phone on.

"We're heading out." Wade was still there. The crowd was starting to disperse. I couldn't see where the other roommates were.

"I'm going to find my own way back. Thanks for inviting me out tonight."

He frowned a little but nodded. "Okay. Well. I'll catch up with the rest. See you later."

He headed off, and I went to the bathroom. When I was done, the crowd had lessened significantly. Still. I knew it would be a wait, but I couldn't bring myself to turn my phone back on. Because of that, I went over to the door that the players used and slid down to the floor.

I got comfortable.

I didn't have to wait long.

Fifteen minutes later, still sweaty from the game, Cruz Styles found me in the hallway. He'd changed into his Grant West hockey sweats and hoodie. He also had a ball cap pulled low over his forehead, and both his hands were inside his hoodie.

He tapped my foot with one of his and gave me one of those smiles I'd been seeing on the jumbotron all night. "Need a ride?"

"You're supposed to look intimidating for your team pictures."

He frowned but held out a hand.

I put mine in it, and he pulled me up. "Huh?"

"For your pictures." I motioned behind us to where there

was a six-foot mural picture of just him. He was in his hockey gear, holding his stick and smiling wide for the camera. "That doesn't strike fear in anyone. The opposing team comes through here. They look at that and want to be your friend."

"No, no, no. You got it all wrong." We turned for the door. "That smile gets under their skin. They've already come in hearing about me, and then they see that, and they get confused. Some guys want to wipe that smile off my face and others want to be my friend. Then I leave 'em all in the dust when I make the first goal and by then, wham. They're all sorts of fucked up."

I laughed because it wasn't true at all. Cruz was just being Cruz.

He opened the door and I stepped out, knowing which one was his truck and heading there. "You didn't shower?"

He went to the driver's side as I got in the passenger side, and he smirked my way. "What? And forget how hot and both- ered I saw you were up in the stands? Figured we could shower together. You game?"

He sent me a smile as he started the engine, and I couldn't help but smile back because like Miles, Cruz knew the deal. No personal shit.

He knew the rules because he was my not-friend with benefits.

And he was right. Showers with him were the best.

Check out the rest of Hockey With Benefits
or go to www.tijansbooks.com

# ALSO BY TIJAN

Another Christmas novella:

A Kade Christmas

Sports Romance Standalones:

Pine River

Anti-Hero

Hockey With Benefits

Enemies

Teardrop Shot

Hate To Love You

The Not-Outcast

Rich Prick

Latest books:

Pine River

Hockey With Benefits

A Dirty Business (Mafia, Kings of New York Series)

A Cruel Arrangement (Mafia, Kings of New York Series)

Aveke (Fallen Crest novella, standalone)

Fallen Crest and Crew Universe

Fallen Crest/Roussou Universe

Fallen Crest Series

Crew Series

The Boy I Grew Up With (standalone)

Rich Prick (standalone)

Frisco

Series:

Broken and Screwed Series (YA/NA)

Jaded Series (YA/NA suspense)

Davy Harwood Series (paranormal)

Carter Reed Series (mafia)

The Insiders

Mafia Standalones:

Cole

Bennett Mafia

Jonah Bennett

Canary

Paranormal Standalones and Series:

Evil

Micaela's Big Bad

The Tracker

Davy Harwood Series (paranormal)

Young Adult Standalones:

Ryan's Bed

A Whole New Crowd

Brady Remington Landed Me in Jail

College Standalones:

Printed in the USA
CPSIA information can be obtained
at www.ICGtesting.com
JSHW030225170124
55544JS00007B/23